On the Road to Glory

A Western Quest Series Novel

On the Road to Glory

A Western Quest Series Novel

Stephen L. Turner

SUNSTONE
PRESS

SANTA FE

Sunstone books may be purchased for educational, business, or sales
promotional use. For information please write: Special Markets Department,
Sunstone Press, P.O. Box 2321, Santa Fe, New Mexico 87504-2321.

Book and Cover design › Vicki Ahl
Body typeface › Book Antiqua
Printed on acid free paper

Library of Congress Cataloging-in-Publication Data

Turner, Stephen L., 1957-
    On the road to glory : a western quest series novel / by Stephen L. Turner.
        p. cm. -- (Western quest ; 5)
    ISBN 978-0-86534-794-6 (pbk. : alk. paper)
1. Confederate States of America. Army--Fiction. 2. Boys--Fiction. 3. United
States--History--Civil War, 1861-1865--Fiction. I. Title.
    PS3620.U76596O6 2011
    813'.6--dc22
                                        2010050694

Published in

WWW.SUNSTONEPRESS.COM
SUNSTONE PRESS / POST OFFICE BOX 2321 / SANTA FE, NM 87504-2321 /USA
(505) 988-4418 / ORDERS ONLY (800) 243-5644 / FAX (505) 988-1025

Dedication

       On the Road to Glory is dedicated to the memory of those Texas heroes, John Bell Hood, Patrick Cleburne, Hiram Granbury and Lawrence Sullivan "Sul" Ross who led the men of Texas in this great conflict. It is also dedicated to the memory of those men who are not widely known, but are heroes in their own right, specifically the Texas Fifteenth Cavalry Regiment, Dismounted, who were part of Granbury's immortal Texas Brigade. It is to their memory, especially Captain Benjamin Tyus and the men of Company F, that this book is dedicated.

Foreword

THE FIRST BOOK IN THE Western Quest Series, *Out of the Wilderness*, follows Thomas Turner as he left Ireland and settled in the wilderness of South Carolina along the Pee Dee River. Book two, *On the Camino Real*, book three, *Under Troubled Skies*, and book four, *Ride for the Lone Star*, follow the life and times of Thomas Turner's grandson, Aaron Turner.

Book five, *On the Road to Glory*, introduces Aaron Turner's youngest son, Aaron Lloyd Turner. Young Aaron leaves home with his brothers, David and Noah, and his brother-in-law, Pinckney Hawkins, to join the Confederacy in turning back the Yankee invasion. He naively believes that it will be a grand adventure as they ride out on the road to glory.

The story is told through the eyes of Aaron who is only ten as the story opens and a war hardened fifteen year old at the end of the conflict. Confederate service records, journals and books accurately locate Aaron in time and place.

He was a courier in the Fifteenth Texas Cavalry Regiment, Dismounted, Company F. He served under Captain Benjamin Tyus for the duration of the war. His regiment was part of what was to be known as Granbury's Texas Brigade under Brigadier General Hiram Granbury. Granbury's Brigade was an integral part of Major General Patrick Cleburne's Division. For much of the war,

Cleburne's Division was part of Lieutenant General Hardee's Corp, which was part of the Army of Tennessee. The Army of Tennessee was variously commanded by General Braxton Bragg, General Joe Johnston, and General John Bell Hood.

Pains have been taken to follow the details and timeline of the war as closely as possible. While the commanding officers, from generals to Captain Tyus, are actual historic figures, Lieutenant Kinney and the men of the First Platoon are fictional. This is the very unit in which Aaron, Noah, David and Pinckney served. The names of the rest of the company have been changed from those actually on the roster to fictional characters to facilitate telling the story. It is in the details of action, thought and emotion that this work becomes historical fiction.

Historians agree that the Battle of Franklin, Tennessee, was one of the bloodiest encounters of the entire war as far as percentage of men lost. Many also believe that the casualties there were due to unnecessary aggression. After the Battle of Franklin, the Army of Tennessee was but a ghost of a fighting unit, and ceased to pose a meaningful threat to the Union.

The war changed Aaron in a way that even he did not understand. But the fiery furnace of the war produced a self-reliant, honest, respected man of tremendous character. In 1938, at age eighty-eight, Aaron attended the Seventy-fifth Reunion of Surviving Union and Confederate Veterans held at Gettysburg, Pennsylvania. It seems that after that event, he finally made peace with the memories that had haunted him for seventy-five years.

Acknowledgements

THANKS ARE DUE TO the custodians of Confederate records at Hill College in Hillsboro, Texas, and the Texas State Archives in Austin. Martha Hertzog, President of the Hood's Texas Brigade Association, was able to provide me with invaluable direction and retrieval of records in Austin. My dear cousin, Ella Turner Bullard, granddaughter of Aaron Lloyd Turner, deserves my thanks for her careful preservation and generous sharing of family history. My wife, Roberta Lyles Turner, and my two married children, Melissa Turner DeBusk, and Aaron Lyles Turner, were patient and supportive. My parents, Doctor Aaron Lynn and Doris Alene Combs Turner, deserve thanks for their meticulous proofreading. Thanks also go to my publisher, Sunstone Press of Santa Fe, New Mexico.

1

March 1, 1860, Navasota Crossing, Texas

THE BACK DOOR SLAMMED so hard it rattled the dishes in the kitchen and woke me from a troubled sleep in my room upstairs. Lige was back.

A belligerent voice boomed through the house. "By God, woman, where are you?"

My stepfather, deep in corn liquor, was home and in a drunken rage again. My father, Aaron Turner, had died nine years ago when I was only one. He left my mother, Nancy, a widow with three sons and a daughter. He had also left her a prosperous store, some choice farm land, and large herd of horses, mules and good quality cattle.

Two years ago my mother had married Lige Campbell. Lige was a widower with one son and a rundown small farm near the river. He could be nice enough when he was sober, but a terror when he was drunk.

I was ten. My brother and best friend, Noah, was twelve. My big brother, David, was eighteen. I really looked up to him, and he was very good to me. My sister, Mary Ann, was fifteen. We got along pretty well and she really helped Mother a lot. My half brothers, Marcus and Lucius, were both married and lived about fifteen miles away in Limestone County, as did my half sister, Louisa and her husband. We had the same mother, but had been born to another father who had died when they were little.

Lige had a seventeen year old son named Cain. He was just as sorry as his father. He wouldn't work and loved to stir up trouble for my brothers and me every chance he got. Sometimes he would deliberately leave a gate open, then we would get blamed when the stock got out, or tear something up to make it look like we had done it. I couldn't stand him, but wasn't big enough to do much about it. But David could, and did, any time Cain gave him a reason. Cain was scared of David, because he knew David could whip him any day of the week and twice on Sundays.

Things had not gone well from the beginning. Lige drank too much, too often. When he drank, he got mean. At first, he would just yell and cuss at Momma and us kids. But soon he did more than yell. That's when the hitting began. He would grab Noah or me by the throat or the arm and whip us with a thick hickory branch for little or no reason. When Momma tried to stop him, he would turn on her. I had hated him since the first time he slapped her. I don't mean that I just didn't like the man; I wished he was dead and that I was big enough to do something about it.

He would sober up and apologize to Mother for what he had done. Then he'd work real hard around the place and in the fields. But sooner or later, he would get drunk again and it would all start over. Mother had taken to sleeping upstairs with Mary Ann. She kept the door locked to keep him out. Tonight, Lige was looking for her.

Angry, drunken feet stomped up the wooden stairs. Noah and I got up and met David in the hallway.

"Woman, open this door now!"

"Lige Campbell, you get out of my house right now or I'm sending for the sheriff!"

Lige tried the door, but found it locked. He kicked the door until the wood splintered and swung open. Momma stood there with a loaded revolver pointed at him. Mary Ann was screaming in the corner.

Before Momma had a chance to use it, he knocked the gun out of her hands and slapped her hard across the face. We had all we were going to take from Lige Campbell.

David sent Noah to fetch Tanner Moore, the sheriff. He grabbed Lige's arm before he could hit Momma again. The old drunk wheeled and hit David a round house punch square in the face with a work hardened fist. He lunged for Momma, but David swung his feet and knocked Lige's legs out from under him, leaving him flat on his back on the floor. He fell backward in the hall, staggering to his feet at the top of the stairs.

"I'm fixin' to kill you, Davey boy!" He reached for his sheath knife, which had fallen to the floor.

"Papa, no!" Cain yelled from the end of the hall.

As Lige bent to pick up the knife, I ran into him as hard as I could, knocking him down the stairs. His head smacked the kitchen floor like an over-ripe pumpkin. My blood was up. I bolted down the stairs and began to pelt his face with my fists.

Cain headed down the stairs to help Lige, but David hit him in the temple and laid him out flat in the hall. I had grown tired of using my fists on Lige. I grabbed a piece of oak stove wood and went to whacking him.

"Aaron! Aaron, stop! You'll kill him! Stop! He's had enough." Davey grabbed my arms and held me back. I started crying like a baby. "Come on. Help me drag him out of the house; he's getting blood on Momma's floor."

We dragged his unconscious carcass out the back door. Cain came behind us, holding his face and breathing threats. "You'll shut your fool mouth and stay out of the way, Cain Campbell, or we'll give you a dose of what your daddy got." Cain backed off because he knew Davey meant it. Momma came down with an angry red whelp on her left cheek.

"Cain, you are to get your father's and your own belongings, and move into the old Teel cabin at the end of the stables. If he ever comes back in my home like this again, I'll kill him." I had never seen Momma so angry or more serious.

Sheriff Moore arrived behind the house with Noah. He had known my parents since he was just a boy. "Miss Nancy, looks like Lige has been at it again. What happened? Did he fall down the stairs again? Any of the rest of you hurt?"

Mother smoothed her night gown and struggled to regain her dignity. "Nothing that won't heal in time, Tanner. Cain and his father will be moving into the old Teel cabin tonight. Would you make sure they get there safely?"

"Yes, Ma'am. It is not my place to be tellin' you what to do, but aren't you ready to get rid of the mean old drunk? Everyone knows how worthless he is."

"Tanner, you know how hard it is to get a divorce. If he stays in the other cabin and tends the farm, maybe it will be alright."

Lige groaned and started to stir on the ground. He had wet himself. His face was a bloody mess. The sheriff and Cain helped him to his feet and walked him the twenty yards to the vacant cabin.

A polecat can't change his stripes, and Lige Campbell would not change his ways. It was not the last misery he would deal our family.

Besides running the store, my mother was also our school teacher. Noah and I still attended, but Mary Ann and David had been out for a while. After my father had died, there hadn't been another Methodist minister, so we all attended the Baptist services. I worked at the store unless there was farm work that needed doing.

At school and the store I heard the adults talking about slavery, states' rights and secession. We didn't own any slaves; nobody at Navasota Crossing did. There was an old black man who worked for Cody Teel on his farm, but they told me he was free.

We had two families that farmed our place for wages. The Chavez family had six children old enough to work the fields. The Lucio family had seven children. Momma told me that they had lived on our place since Aaron Chavez and Angelo Lucio were about twelve years old. My father had rescued them from the Comanche. Mr. Chavez could read and write very well. He studied the law with one of the local attorneys when the farm work permitted it.

We had friends over on the Brazos who had big farms with slaves. The largest farm was called the Applewhite Plantation for the man who had started it. His descendants farmed it now. I guess I didn't know or care enough about slaves to have an opinion, but the adults could get pretty worked up about it.

As far as states' rights, Mother had taught us at school that the Tenth Amendment to the United States Constitution reserved all rights to the states not specifically given to the national government. She said the states had freely entered the Union and could freely leave it, too. I think I could understand that. I know that folks in Texas didn't care much for politicians in Washington telling Texans what to do.

The part I didn't understand was when people started talking about secession. I didn't even know what that word meant until I asked Mother. She said it would be a state deciding it didn't want to be part of the United States anymore and going on its own. Now that seemed like a durned fool idea to me. There had just been a war fought because Texas joined up with the Union. Why would anybody want to get out?

My family was friends with Sam Houston. He was Governor of Texas right now. But he had been a United States Senator and President of the Republic of Texas. We all set a lot of store by Houston's opinions. I heard Sheriff Moore telling that Texas had no business ever pulling out of the Union. He had fought with my father and some of the other local men in the war between the United States and Mexico in 1846. He told me he had lost one of the best friends he ever had in that war. But not everyone shared his views, and sheriff of Leon County was an elected position, so he didn't say much. Well, if Sam Houston and the sheriff both felt that way, I guess that settled for me.

———

A stack of newspapers came in from Austin for us to sell at the store. The sheriff bought one, sat on the porch and lit his pipe. He got to talking to Logan Morgan who had stopped by to pick up a keg of nails. I sat down on the porch, just close enough that I could hear them, but far enough they wouldn't notice I was listening.

"Says here, Logan, the Democrat Party has split over slavery. There's a Northern Democrat Party and a Southern Democrat Party. They're both runnin' somebody different for President."

"Who are they runnin'? Anybody we know?"

The sheriff shuffled the paper. "Yes, here it is. The Southerners are runnin' John Breckenridge from Kentucky. The Northerners are puttin' up that blow hard Stephen Douglas from Illinois. He's weak on states' rights, hates slavery, and says anybody who talks about secession is a traitor."

"He's that fella from Illinois that made such a stir debatin' that other character from Illinois, Abraham Lincoln. Can't say as I like either one of 'em."

"Well, I betcha they wouldn't like you either. Remember about four years ago when they started that new Republican Party?"

"Yeah, I remember. Who are they runnin'?"

"Abraham Stinkin' Lincoln! He's the worst of 'em. Against states' rights, in favor of a strong Union, and about as anti-southern as anybody. Lord, I hope we don't get stuck with him as President!"

"What's the ol' 'Raven' got to say about all this? Anything Sam Houston says is good as gospel."

"He's joined a new party called the Constitutional Union Party. They are puttin' up somebody called John Bell from Tennessee. They support states' rights, leavin' slavery alone, but not lettin' it spread, and are against secession."

"With that many people slicin' the political pie, it's liable to get real interestin' this fall."

I tried to soak it all in. It was too complex for my ten year old mind. If Sam Houston liked the Constitutional Union Party, I guess I did, too.

We plowed and planted corn, cotton, ribbon cane, black-eyed peas, Irish potatoes, sweet potatoes, other vegetables and a small patch of tobacco. Lige and Cain showed up every day and worked hard enough, I suppose. Ol' Lige was always hollering at one of us boys, or one of the Mexicans, about something. We mostly just ignored him and went about our business.

David had been courting a local sixteen year old girl named Alma. She was sure pretty and sweet. We teased him a lot about her, but we liked Alma real well. Our sister, Mary Ann, was fifteen. She was sweet on a young man from Personville over in Limestone County. His name was Pinckney Hawkins. He was a nice man and a hard worker, with a farm, some livestock and a good cabin. He was respectful to Momma and my sister. Momma liked him well enough, but was a little worried that he was ten years older than Mary Ann. I thought Pinckney was a mighty peculiar name. We called him "Pink," but he didn't seem to mind.

By the time we had cut the wheat and oats, and the corn and cotton were up to a good stand, David had asked Alma to marry him. Within a week, Pinckney had popped the question to Mary Ann. Noah and I made smooching sounds behind their backs and giggled.

My father had been a Methodist minister, but I didn't remember him at all. Noah, David, and Mary Ann told me lots of things about him. Everyone said I looked a lot like him. Momma told me stories about him all the time. He had been the one who founded Navasota Crossing. She told me he was a very good man, kind and giving, and had been a natural leader. He had been a brave man, too, having fought British soldiers, pirates, Indians, bandits, and Mexican soldiers. She got a pension from the United States Army for his having served as a Colonel of Scouts in the Mexican War. The adults around the settlement told me what a fine man he had been. He had been the commanding officer for most of the men around those parts in the Texas militia. Everybody said he had a good sense of humor and enjoyed a good laugh. I wished that I had known him. The stepfather in my life wasn't worth the powder and lead it would take to shoot him. If he was on fire, I wouldn't pee on him to put it out.

David, and to a lesser extent, Marcus and Lucius, stepped in where and when a man was needed by Noah or me. David had told me all I wanted to know about growing up from a boy into a man. That liked to have embarrassed him to death. I didn't tell him I had that part pretty well figured out from having two older brothers in the house. I just listened and blushed, while he talked to me just like I was his own kid. He had to do the "birds and the bees talk," too. Growing up around a herd of livestock, I kind of already had that pretty well figured out, too. I think that talk was harder on Davey than it was on me, mostly because I kept giggling and snorting like a bull. He was the closest thing I had to a father, even though he was only eight years older than me.

Now, Noah was the best friend I had in the world. We had shared a bed since I was old enough to remember. I went everywhere he went and did everything he did, or died trying. He wouldn't have let anybody hurt me for anything, but that didn't stop us from dusting things up pretty good sometimes between ourselves. And I'll guarantee you nobody was going to hurt Noah if I had a way to stop it.

My mother was the best mother in the whole world. She was so good to us, and always let us know she loved us. She would sit out on the porch and read to us when we were little from the Bible and from storybooks. She'd patch us up when we got hurt, and take a switch to us if we needed that, too. She taught us to respect grownups and to be polite to women and old folks. She didn't hold with tobacco or alcohol "used to excess." Once in a while Noah and I would try a little chewing tobacco, but never really cared for it. When nobody was looking, we would sneak a little sip of the corn liquor Lige thought he had hidden in the hay loft. We knew all the cuss words, but almost never let one slip, except under extreme conditions, like the milk cow stepping in the bucket or getting thrown off a horse. Momma would just clear her throat if she heard it, just to make sure we remembered our manners.

In August, there was a huge double wedding at Navasota Crossing. David and Alma got married at the same time as Pinckney and Mary Ann. Folks from all around came to the wedding. The Baptist minister officiated at the biggest wedding I had ever seen. He got everybody started off by singing hymns just like a Sunday morning. Our little church didn't have a piano, so we just sang out of the *Sacred Selections*. I'd have thought two hymns would have been plenty, but he had wheezed through four songs with all the verses, before he had the first prayer. That preacher prayed so long, I fell asleep and got elbowed by Momma. Then the wedding part got started, and the two grooms walked in and waited up front while the two brides walked down the aisle. There was another long prayer before he started preaching. Now that preacher must have thought he was getting paid by the hour, but I swear to goodness, he fired up in Genesis and worked his way clear through to Revelation before they even got to the "I Do" part. By then, I didn't much care if they did or didn't, as long as old "Brother Blabbermouth" just finished up. I thought he was about to wind it up when he launched into "The plan of Salvation," gave an altar call and offered to baptize or pray for all of us sinners. The white starched collar on my Sunday shirt was rubbing my neck and sweat rolled down my back. Noah kept passing a little gas and got me to giggling, which resulted in a hard thump to my head by Momma. I sure was glad when it was ended.

After the ceremony was finally over, we threw seed over the newlyweds' heads. Noah and I raced each other home to change clothes. Angelo Lucio had butchered a couple of corn-fed steers. He had been slowly cooking the meat over smoking oak coals all day long. We could smell the meat cooking from the house. He had cooked large black kettles of pinto beans until they were falling apart tender. There were too many folks to feed with cornbread, so Angelo's wife had made huge stacks of fresh corn tortillas. Ripe watermelons were lined up in the shade ready to eat for dessert. We ate until we were about to bust.

The local musicians pulled out their fiddles and guitars and started tuning up to play. One fellow even had a banjo. By the time the evening cooled down, the music heated up. There was dancing all up and down the street. Momma danced a little with David, and once or twice with Marcus and Lucius. She talked me into dancing once with her, and so did Mary Ann and Alma.

By the time the lightning bugs came out in the trees along the river, the crocks of whiskey started showing up at the back of the crowd so as to not be too noticeable. Of course, my stepfather was one of the first to tip back a jug. That would mean trouble for our family again before the night was over.

———

The party started winding down about midnight. The new couples left to their destinations in borrowed buggies. The musicians put up their instruments and everyone headed home. Lige was loud and obnoxious. He followed us home and pushed his way inside.

"Lige, you don't belong here. Get to your own cabin. Now, Lige!"

"Woman, don't you take that tone with me. I'm yore husband and I'm stayin' here tonight." He reared back and slapped Momma in the face.

I knew Noah and I couldn't handle him with David gone. I had an idea. I ran to the well and pulled up a stoneware crock suspended by a rope in the well. I ran to the kitchen with the jug.

"Look, Lige. I brung ya another jug!"

"Give me that, you snot-nosed brat."

He yanked the jug out of my hands and began to guzzle the whiskey. One predictable thing about Lige, he didn't stop drinking until he got to the bottom of the bottle. In half an hour he had passed out in the downstairs bedroom, snoring like a bear. Momma had Noah and me help her roll the old drunk up in a blanket. She used strong cotton thread to sew him up good and tight. We couldn't figure out what she was doing when she came back into the bedroom with a broom. She proceeded to beat the devil out of that old buzzard with the broomstick. The louder he hollered, the harder she hit him. When she finally got tired, she handed us the broom and let us get in a few good licks.

We helped her drag him out of the house, still rolled up in the blanket and still hollering. Cain heard the racket and came trotting over to see what we were doing. I ran into the house and grabbed a Colt Paterson .36 revolver. I leveled it at Cain's belly.

"Cain Campbell, you keep out of this. I'm mad and I'm tired of him hittin' Momma. You git yourself back to your own cabin. You come any closer and I'm gonna blow a hole in ya!" He turned and went slinking like a snake back in to its hole.

Noah had run to get Sheriff Moore. They were back in a few minutes along with Logan Morgan. The two men dragged him to a horse and threw him over the saddle none too gently.

Sheriff Moore walked over to Mother. "You alright, Miss Nancy?"

"Nothing serious, Tanner. Thank you for coming again. This is very embarrassing."

"Ol' Lige musta fallen down the stairs again. It's not surprisin' he fell, tangled up in that blanket like that. Nancy, I've known you since I was ten years old. I'm worried about ya. This isn't gonna end here. I'll help ya file for a divorce."

"I wasn't raised that way, Tanner. I would only divorce him if he were to be unfaithful."

"Seems to me he cheats on ya with the jug. And no man has a right to hit his wife and beat her kids."

"I'll think on it, Sheriff."

Sheriff Moore looked up and saw Cain easing over from his cabin. "Cain, unless you want to spend the night in jail with your ol' daddy, you had better not set foot out of that cabin until daylight."

Lige spent a few days as a guest of Leon County in the sheriff's only jail cell. In spite of our begging, Mother was not ready to divorce him. He was back in his own cabin, meek as a mouse. I knew we had not seen the last trouble from Lige Campbell.

Fall came with cool clear days. Our corn cribs were so full, we had extra to sell. The cotton made a good crop, too. The Chavez and Lucio families had worked side by side with Noah and me pulling the fluffy white cotton out of the dried bolls from daylight to dark. My fingers were chewed up from the tough burrs and my shoulder hurt from dragging the long, heavy sack down the long rows. The fall brought good prices for our cotton, but it brought something much more troubling. This fall brought the election of 1860 that threatened to pull our nation apart.

There hadn't been much speech making in our part of the world. I guess there weren't enough people to make it worth the bother. Nobody was running against Sheriff Moore. But the big issue was the Presidential election. The grownups talked about it all the time. I was sick of hearing about it. I couldn't see how it would affect us here on the Navasota much one way or the other. I was wrong. I was very, very wrong.

When the news finally came that the Republican, Abraham Lincoln, had been elected, a dark mood settled over the adults like the death of a child. I was too busy plowing down the corn stubble to pay attention. From what I know now, looking back at those times, it was best that I was too tired to notice or care. The world as we knew it was about to be torn apart. We were standing on the edge of a nightmare that would touch the lives of every living soul.

2

Spring 1861, Navasota Crossing, Texas

MEN FROM OUR SETTLEMENT and all over Texas had met and voted overwhelmingly to leave the United States. My family was at a loss as to what this would mean. The Texas legislature had proclaimed that all elected officials of the state of Texas must swear allegiance to the still developing Confederate States of America. Our friend, Governor Sam Houston, had declined, and the office of governor had been declared vacant. How could the people of Texas do this to the man who had seen us through the Revolution, held us together during the dark days of the Republic and gained our admission to the United States? It was too much for my eleven year old mind to comprehend.

South Carolina had seceded first. In April 1861, they had opened fire on Fort Sumter in Charleston harbor when the Union garrison refused to surrender. Soon, Mississippi, Florida, Alabama, Georgia and Louisiana had left the Union for the Confederacy. With Texas and South Carolina, they made the circle of seven stars in the blue field on the new Confederate flag, with broad red and white bands, known as the Stars and Bars. The fledgling government had its capital in Montgomery, Alabama.

Arkansas, Tennessee and North Carolina soon followed the rest. When Virginia seceded, the west fifty counties declared their loyalty to the Union, and would later be formed into the state of West Virginia. For reasons I never understood, the Confederacy moved its capital to Richmond, Virginia, within spitting distance of Washington, D.C.

New Mexico and Arizona Territories declared for the Confederacy, as did many of the Indian Nations in the Oklahoma Territory. Maryland, Delaware, Missouri and Kentucky were slave states. Their populations were divided in their loyalties, but stayed in the Union. Missouri and Kentucky had duel governments, both Confederate and Union.

At school and the post office, a new flag flew where the Stars and Stripes had flown since 1846. I shook my head in disbelief. Momma cried and I didn't understand why.

———

David and Alma lived in the cabin in the northeast corner of the stockade where the Moore family had lived years ago. The old snake, Lige, and his rotten son, still lived in the northwest cabin where Father's friend, Nick Teel, had lived before moving farther west. I hated Lige as hard as an eleven year old heart could hate. We all worked the fields together, but Lige and Cain stepped lightly when David was around.

I took a growing spurt that summer. I had always had big hands and feet with long arms and legs, but I was stretching out like pole beans growing up a corn stalk. Looking at my two older brothers at home, I wasn't surprised. I had been hoping to grow, since Noah at thirteen, was already five foot nine inches. Davey was a little over six feet tall. He told me Father had been a tall man, too. Maybe I would finally measure up to my brothers.

———

By summer, Confederate recruiters came through passing out handbills. They brought drummer boys not any older than me to bang away as the recruiters urged all eligible men from fifteen to forty-five to come to the new Leon County seat of Centerville to enlist.

There was lots of excitement as people talked about the war. The young men flocked to Centerville to enlist. Those of us too young to enlist took to playing soldier with sawmill bats as guns and sabers, slaying evil Yankees at every turn.

David was in a dilemma. He still felt it was a mistake for Texas to have left the Union, but it had already happened. He felt a strong loyalty to Texas. He had been born during the days of the Republic. He remembered our father riding off to the Mexican War when Texas had become a state, and he remembered him finally riding home again. Ultimately, it was Alma who influenced his decision the most.

"Davey, you don't have to go atall. Who's gonna run the farm? Who's gonna take care of me? Who's gonna protect yore mother and yore brothers from Lige?"

That clenched it. He couldn't leave home the way things were. Unless Lige Campbell was dead or gone, David would have to stay as long as he needed to.

Men flooded to Centerville to enlist. Mother let Noah and me ride over to see the excitement. They were recruiting for the Texas Fifth Regiment of Infantry under John Bell Hood. They were calling themselves the "Leon Hunters." To our amazement, our good for nothing stepbrother, Cain, enlisted. Mother was happy and ol' Lige had a fit. Hood's Brigade would become known as one of the toughest units in the eastern theater of the war, but at a terrible price in blood and bodies.

_____

In the fall, another recruiting effort was underway for Waul's Texas Legion. Many of those who had not already enlisted did so now. The recruiters were freely passing out corn liquor to encourage the men's patriotism. Lige had seen fit to drown himself in whiskey.

After dark, he came stumbling to our cabin in an alcoholic rage.

"Nancy, open the door! Nancy!"

Mother was not able to get the oak bar dropped into place before he had kicked through the back door into the kitchen. He slapped her hard across the face.

"It's your fault my only boy is gone off to war. If you had been a good mother to him, he would still be here with me."

He struck her again hard across the face. Noah ran to get David and the sheriff. I tried to get myself between him and Momma.

"Git out of my way, you snot-nosed brat!"

"You go to hell, Lige Campbell! You leave Momma alone!"

He punched me in the face and stomach with his fists leaving me doubled over and bleeding on the floor. Momma huddled over me to protect me. He kicked her hard in the ribs. David burst through the door into the kitchen. He unleashed years of fermented anger on his drunken, abusive stepfather. He pounded Lige with all he had, driving him back with every blow. But Lige was strong when he was in liquor, and he hit Davey hard enough to hurt him. The fight came to a sudden conclusion when Momma hit ol' Lige in the head with a cast iron skillet. He went down like a butchered hog. Blood was freely flowing from the back of his head. We dragged him outside and tied him up hand and foot.

He slowly opened his eyes and began to strain at the ropes and cuss a blue streak. I leaned over and punched him in the nose as hard as I could. Blood squirted down his face from his freshly broken nose.

"That was for Momma, and this is for me!" I kicked him in the ribs as hard as I could with my heavy brogans.

Sheriff Moore arrived with Noah, Logan Morgan, and a Confederate Army recruiter. "Well, Lige. Looks like you got drunk and fell down the stairs again. You really should stop drinkin', you know. I've had all I want from you. I'm gonna haul you in and charge you with attempted murder. I got four reliable witnesses, and I'll personally pick the jury when you go to trial. You don't have a friend in Leon County. The jury will send you to rot for the rest of your sorry life in Huntsville prison."

"Attempted murder? All I done was discipline my wife and stepson."

"Is that the way all the rest of you saw it?"

"Sheriff Moore, I believe you have summarized the situation quite well. He tried to kill Aaron and me. Please arrest him. I'll sign the charges and testify against him in court."

"Now just a gall durned minute. I don't stand a chance in a jury trial."

"No, Lige, you don't. I'm offerin' you one chance. You can take it or leave it. This Confederate Recruiting Sergeant is here to enlist you in Waul's Legion. But just so you know, if you ever show your face in Leon County again, I'll shoot you on site as an escaped felon."

"Hell, Sheriff, you don't leave a man no choice atall."

"Sergeant, looks like you have a new recruit. You do shoot deserters don't you?"

"Sure do, Sheriff. I need him to walk along behind my horse, so I'll need to untie his feet. Would you be willin' to help me tie a rope around his waist? You wouldn't mind donatin' a little rope for the good of the cause, would you?"

3

February 1862, Personville, Limestone County, Texas

WE HAD ALL HEARD HOW the South had sent the Yankees running back to Washington from their defeat at Manassas Junction, Virginia. Some people said one Reb could whip a dozen Yankees. Others said the North didn't have the heart to fight. My mother quietly reminded me that my father had fought under the Stars and Stripes at New Orleans and in Mexico. She said to never underestimate the strength and determination of the United States. My brothers and I agreed. But we boasted with our friends like we thought the Yankees had blue backs and yellow bellies. But we quietly shared our doubts among ourselves and with Pink.

"Hey, Pink. Tell my little brothers what the South is facin'."

"The Yankees have got a big Navy with all kinds and sizes of ships and cannon. The South doesn't have a rowboat right now."

"That ain't gonna bother anybody except along the coast." I interrupted.

"Aaron, where does your family get money to buy things you need?"

"We grow what we need."

"Can you grow a rifle, gunpowder or shot? What about coffee?"

"No, you know we buy that stuff with money we get from sellin' cotton, and those danged Yankees ain't got an acre of it."

"The Union Navy is already tryin' to close up all the seaports from Virginia to the Rio Grande. If they get it done, and it looks like they will, we won't be able to sell a bale of cotton, buy a gun or a pound of coffee."

"They can't have that many ships!" Noah argued.

"They've got that many and more. They've got factories that can make anything from a plow to cannon. For any one item the South can manufacture, they can make twenty. They have twelve miles of railroad tracks for every single mile of Southern track."

"Why are you tellin' all this anyhow, Pink?" I asked irritably.

"Because this war is gonna be long and hard. Anyone who says otherwise doesn't know his facts."

"You gonna fight for the South, Pink?" David asked quietly.

"Here, ya'll read this handbill. They're recruitin' this weekend at Personville over in Limestone County. I've already talked to Mary Ann. She thinks I should go."

David looked down at the floor. "I've already talked to Alma. I'm enlistin', too."

A strange twisting sensation took hold of me like a large cold hand squeezing my guts. This war had just gotten real personal. I felt like I had the chills and wanted to puke.

I had a lot of things on my mind. Noah and I lay in bed and talked late into the night.

"Aaron, I wanna to go with David and Pink."

"I do, too, but whose gonna look after Momma?"

"Davey says Alma and Mary Ann are gonna move back in here when he leaves. He said Chavez and Lucio can take care of the livestock and the farm with some supervision from Momma. Lucius and Marcus only live fifteen miles from here and can help, too."

Marcus and Lucius were Momma's sons from her first marriage. Their father had died in the War of 1812. When she and Father married, he had raised them like his own. They were twenty years older than Noah and me. They were good men who loved our Momma and had always been real good to us, too.

"What if that ol' snake Lige Campbell shows up around here?"

"Well, I reckon Sheriff Moore would shoot him, but I'm still studyin' on that part, too."

I lay quietly in the bed Logan Morgan had built, under a cotton quilt Momma had made. Noah, my brother and best friend, had finally fallen asleep. I didn't want to leave home, but I sure didn't want to be separated from Noah and David. I decided if Noah figured out a way to join up, I was going with him.

I was unloading a freight wagon at the store when a boy about my age rode up on a tall horse. The boy wasn't nearly as big as me, but he was wearing a gray Confederate uniform with a couriers pouch strapped to his side.

"I have a letter for Mrs. Lige Campbell."

"That's my mother. Let me git her."

Momma and Noah came out on the porch while the messenger dug a folded envelope out of the pouch. He handed it to Momma, tipped his hat and rode away. It was chilly out on the porch, so we stepped inside the store. Momma pulled up a wooden crate and sat down by the big black potbelly stove. She read the letter and put a hand to her forehead with a strange look on her face.

"Boys, Lige is dead. He took sick and died of dysentery about a month ago near Houston."

"The ol' drunk died of the runs? Hallelujah!"

"Aaron, you hush that."

"Aren't you glad, Momma?" I asked.

"Not exactly. But I'm not sad, either. He has hung over this family like a black cloud for a long time. I feel like a burden has been taken away." She smiled and clutched the letter. "He's not ever coming back to bother us again."

I went back to unloading the wagon; the teamster would be back pretty soon and would not want to be waiting on me to finish my work. I was whistling and happier than I had been in awhile. I guess it was wrong to be glad anybody was dead, especially an old sinner like Lige who was roasting in Hell right now. But there was no doubt about it, I was glad the old drunk was dead.

Noah came out and began helping unload the wagon. "Aaron, that letter is a sure enough sign that it is alright for us to leave Momma. The only thing holdin' us back was wonderin' if Lige might come back and hurt Mother. Nobody comes back from where he is now. I'm goin' with Davey and Pink, and takin' you along, too."

Mother had given us a good long, logical argument on all the reasons why Noah and I ought not to go with David and Pink. But she never said we couldn't go. She agreed to let us ride to Personville and talk to the recruiters. I think she was convinced they wouldn't let us join up because of our ages. Noah was only fourteen and I was just twelve. But Noah was six feet tall and as strong as most men. I was already five foot nine inches. Nobody was going to mistake us for adults, but it was worth a try.

———

Noah, David, Pink and I left at dawn for the two and a half hour ride to Marcus' home in Personville. The morning air was crisp and fresh. I could feel the excitement as we rode. My mouth was dry and my hands were sweating in spite of the cool weather.

We left our horses at Marcus' house and walked the short distance down the road with him to the tavern he and his wife ran. They fixed us a good breakfast and a pot of strong coffee. We passed the time visiting with Marcus at one of the tables as other customers and potential recruits drifted in and warmed themselves by the stove.

Just before noon, four men in gray uniforms tied their horses to the rail in front of the tavern. They sat at a corner table and ordered the house lunch. After they had eaten, a sergeant who appeared to be the leader of the group stood up and stretched. His uniform was perfect. The brass buttons shone like gold. He carried a revolver in a flap-top holster and a shining sword. He pulled a rag from his pocket and wiped the road dust from his knee high boots.

"I'm Sergeant Joe Barnett. I'm here lookin' for men to defend our state from the Yankees. You haven't seen any of them yet, but they're all along the coast with their navy, and their armies are formin' up back east. We're going to stop them before they ever set foot on the sacred soil of Texas. I need men who can shoot. I need men who are willin' to raise arms in defense of our homes and families. We are gatherin' up a regiment to ride on the road to glory and whip those Yankees all the way back North. If any of you is that kind of patriotic man, come and talk to me, or to one of these young men with me. This is my son, Private Ethan Barnett, Corporal Harold Payton, and his brother, Private Bradley Payton."

The four of them worked the crowd. The privates and the corporal were just as well dressed as the sergeant. Noah and I stood in awe of the soldiers. The sergeant wandered up and looked us over.

"How old are you two boys?"

"My name is Aaron Turner, I'm fifteen. This here is my brother, Noah, he's sixteen."

"Well, Aaron, what year were you born?"

"I was born in 1850…" I knew I had been caught.

"And you, Noah?"

"I was born in '48."

"You boys are a little rusty on your math. I believe that would make you twelve and you fourteen, now wouldn't it? You come back and see me in a year or two if the war ain't over by then."

"Wait, Sergeant. We can do anythin' those soldier boys you got with ya, and probably do it better!"

"Well, aren't you a feisty one. You figure out a way to back that up, and we'll talk."

David and Pink just shook their heads at us, but Noah and I took off at a trot for Marcus' house to get our horses, rifles and revolvers. In a few minutes, we were back at the tavern, saddled up out front.

"Hey, Sergeant Barnett? Sergeant?"

Sergeant Barnett, the other three soldiers, Pink, David and Marcus stepped out onto the porch along with a dozen other men. "What can I do for you boys?" he said with a grin.

"Sergeant, you let us race your troopers and take 'em on in a little shootin' match. If we can hold up our end, will you at least think about recruitin' us?"

"Tell you what I'll do, Aaron. If you can live up to all that cocky braggin', I'll personally take it up with Captain Tyus. That's the best I can do."

He described the route for a horse race to start and end at the tavern. The cavalry horses looked fresh and good quality. But I knew ours were better. The crack of his .44 Colt set us surging forward. All five horses were pretty well neck to neck until we got to the creek. Our well-bred Thoroughbred crosses took the creek in two great bounds. Once across, light rein and spur pressure spun them racing north a full length ahead of the cavalrymen.

At the large oak tree that marked our next turn we wheeled back east. A large limb had fallen across the path. Our horses vaulted the limb without breaking stride. One cavalry horse cleared the branch. Another balked, then jumped over it with all the grace of a hog jumping a puddle. The third horse skidded to a halt and refused to cross. The remaining two troopers spurred their mounts in an effort to catch us. Once we turned on the Personville Road, we gave our horses their heads and touched them with our spurs. They responded like champions with a powerful surge of speed. They thundered ahead, reaching the tavern six lengths ahead of the soldiers. The men at the tavern cheered our victory, even Sergeant Barnett. Once the last trooper tied his horse, we prepared for our shooting challenge.

One of the men set up several empty bottles in the street and marked a line in the dirt at twenty paces. The soldiers would shoot first. They carried .44 caliber Colt Navy revolvers. They each hit three out of six shots.

"Sergeant, we're just kids so we wanna make this fair." I stepped off an additional ten paces from the remaining bottles. We both carried our father's old Colt Paterson five shot revolvers in .36 caliber. We took our time and both hit five for five. There was clapping and whistling from the porch. "Y'all ready to see what we can do with a rifle?"

"I give up. You boys have shown me enough. I'm gonna talk to Captain Tyus. With a hundred like you, we could take Washington in week! I'm gonna take a little liberty with your ages. Can y'all keep your mouths shut about it? I'll see you back here in a week. Bring those good horses, your revolvers, and rifles. Git somebody to run you up a uniform and a war bag with the rest of your stuff."

_____

Momma made uniforms for Noah and me, while Mary Ann and Alma sewed them for David and Pink. We each had a pair of sturdy plain gray pants. She made Noah's and mine extra long to allow for us to grow. We each had a gray cotton waistcoat with plain buttons and a gray wool cape. We each got two white cotton shirts, two pairs of cotton drawers and two pair of long woolen drawers, three pairs of wool socks, plus locally made heavy brogans and black belts. Momma gave each of us a pistol. David and Pink got the huge .44 Walker Colts. Noah and I were given the .36 caliber Paterson Colt five shot revolvers. All four of us got .50 caliber Springfield rifles that she had traded for at the store. She fixed each of us an oiled leather war bag. They each contained our extra clothes, a few bars of lye soap, a tin cup, bowl and plate, plus some utensils, a poke of salt, a little coffee, a pencil and note pad, and a small Bible. She had fixed us bedrolls made of heavy wool blankets inside heavyweight waterproof canvas. The canvas had leather straps to roll it up tight behind the saddle.

Sheriff Moore and Cody Teel went out with us to pick just the right horses to take with us from our herd. Stallions and mares could be unpredictable. We knew geldings would be best. Too tall a horse might have trouble in close quarters, while a short one might not be able to keep up. We finally settled on four stout geldings of about fifteen hands each, with good clean feet and deep chests. Mine was a good bay called Wichita.

I was as ready for war as a twelve year old could be. I dreamed of charging into fleeing lines of retreating Yankees and driving them back north. In a few months, my dreams of the golden road to glory would seem more like the tortured nightmares of hell.

———————

The day of enlistment arrived. All of us said our goodbyes on the front porch of the houses in the breaking dawn. David and Alma held each other like they would never see each other again. It was just as bad with Pink and Mary Ann. Noah and I hugged our sister and Momma. I clung to her just a little too long and we both had tears rolling down our faces. I gave her a kiss on the cheek and climbed on Wichita. We turned west on the rutted Camino Real and splashed across the ford on the Navasota. A cold hand gripped my heart, and my breath came short and tight, but I would not look back. I was riding off to war with my brothers.

The excitement in the air reached our ears before our eyes. We could hear a military band playing "The Yellow Rose of Texas" amid cheering voices. As we rode into Personville, we saw Sergeant Barnett and his recruiting detail on the porch of Marcus' tavern. We climbed down and tied our horses.

"Mornin' Sergeant! You still want all four of us?"

"Yes, all four of you, David. Corporal Payton, run get Captain Tyus."

A thin man of medium height and gray hair walked out on the porch. He was dressed in a fine gray uniform with brass buttons and gold braid. He looked at us through intense pale blue eyes, inspecting us from head to toe. "Sergeant Barnett has already spoken to me about you. Swear 'em in, Sergeant." He turned on his heel and quickly walked away.

We were administered an oath of loyalty to Texas and the Confederacy and signed into the company books by Quartermaster Sergeant Matthews. "This is the Texas Fifteenth Cavalry Regiment, Company F. Captain Tyus is your commanding officer. You'll be in First Platoon, First Squad, under Lieutenant Kinney and Sergeant Kyle Howard. Report to the livery stable and you'll be given the rest of your gear."

We grinned with pride as we untied our horses and led them to the livery. The Quartermaster Sergeant walked over there with us. He was young, about six feet tall with reddish hair and blue eyes. "You boys have brought good horses. They'll be yours to ride and keep. The Confederacy will reimburse you $50 for your horse if it's killed, captured, or rendered unfit for service at the time of your discharge. You'll be reimbursed forty cents a day for upkeep of your horse. These saddles will do nicely. The Confederacy will replace them if necessary. I see you have your war bags and bedrolls. The private here will get each of you army forage caps and ammunition for your weapons.

"Which one of you is Aaron? You? Here's your courier pouch for messages. It's waterproof, but not bulletproof." The quartermaster paused, then realized I had not caught his joke.

"Pinckney Hawkins? You? You've been assigned as a teamster to drive the assistant surgeon's wagon. You'll fight with First Platoon, First Squadron. Any questions? Then move along, boys, move along."

"I'm Private Taylor Edwards. Glad to meet ya'll. I'm gonna be fittin' ya for your forage caps." He stepped forward and shook hands with each of us. He was about sixteen, and his eyes spoke the potential for mischief. He measured around our heads and gave us the appropriate size caps. They were sharp looking gray wool with black leather bills and a brass "CSA" emblem on the front. "Y'all are supposed to go find Lieutenant Kinney now. I'll be seein' y'all!"

We walked by Marcus' tavern to show off our new uniforms to him. He made all the right remarks about how good we looked. We each had a large bowl of beef stew and cornbread for an early lunch.

"Yonder comes your Lieutenant Kinney and his son. You best look sharp and see what he wants you to do."

A lean man, over six feet tall, with thinning hair and gray eyes walked into the tavern. His quick eyes missed nothing.

"Lieutenant Kinney, sir?" David asked.

"Yes, son? What can I do for you?"

"We've been assigned to your platoon, sir."

"Well, good! At least they're not all outlaws, drunks and midgets! Welcome to Company F, First Platoon. Private Kinney will show you where to billet."

Private Kinney was his son, Trent, of about sixteen or seventeen. He looked like a younger version of his father except for blond hair. He was wearing the nicest uniform I ever saw a private wear anywhere; it looked like it belonged to a general or something, except it didn't have all the gold lace and such. He had big feet, and reached out with big hands to shake with each of us.

"I'm Trent. I'm supposed to be an aide for my pa. Mostly that means runnin' errands and tryin' to stay out of the way. Come on, I'll take you over to the camp and introduce y'all to Sergeant Howard."

He led us to a grove of live oak trees along the little creek where we had recently raced west of Personville. The new company was starting to take shape there. "This is Sergeant Kyle Howard. There's a whole bunch of Howards in our platoon, either his sons or his nephews."

We made a round of introductions, in awe of everything we saw. "Nice to meet you boys. Let's see, here. You must be Aaron; you're supposed to be the courier. You stick close to me to carry messages back and forth to the lieutenant. He may send you all the way on up to regimental headquarters, so you keep your horse handy, saddled and ready to ride. Pinckney? Do they call ya 'Pink'? You're part of this platoon and squadron. You'll bed down, mess and fight with us. But when we are on the road, you'll be a teamster for Doc Wade, the assistant surgeon. David, you and Noah will have regular duties in the platoon. We'll git along real good." He smiled a crooked smile and spit tobacco juice at a beetle crawling along the ground. "Y'all picket your horses down by the creek. Aaron, groom your horse, then resaddle him. You can loosen the cinches, but keep him saddled."

We did like we had been told. I carefully groomed Wichita, rubbed his back, then carefully resaddled him with partially tightened cinches. Corporal Hamilton Howard came by.

"Y'all met my Daddy, the sergeant. Everybody just calls me Ham, since Hamilton is too long." He shook hands with all of us, and you could see he was making an effort to learn all our names. He was well over six feet tall with shoulders as broad as a barn door and a smile to match. "Let me introduce y'all to my brothers. This skinny one is the oldest. His name is Hezekiah, but everybody calls him Ky. The big one there is Skeet; he's the baby." Ham had been right about Ky being skinny, but he was real friendly to us. The baby brother, Skeet, was blond headed with blue eyes. All the rest were dark headed with dark eyes. He had dimples that would catch rainwater. He wasn't quite as tall as Ham, but he had shoulders on him so wide and thick, I believe he could have tied horseshoes into pretzels with his bare hands. They had two cousins there, too. Lath was scrawny and wiry built. Tobe was middlin' tall and dark as a storm cloud.

The Howard bunch helped us get our tent up. It was a little more complicated than I would have guessed, but they were patient to show us how to do it right. Later that evening, Sergeant Howard came by with Taylor Edwards and another private, Brandon Moss. We had met Taylor when we got our caps. Brandon was a big kid, about fifteen, strong, quiet and plenty smart. They would be sharing our tent and cooking.

Skeet came along later and brought us a medium sized skillet, a tin coffee pot, a Dutch oven, a poke of cornmeal, a sack of coffee, and some smoked side meat. It would be plain country eating like most of us had at home every day.

———

We had just finished cleaning up after supper when Sergeant Howard came along. "Captain Tyus has called a company meetin'.

Gather over there by the picket line and stay together. He is a good man, so all of you mind your manners."

Captain Tyus stood out away from the creek where he could face the various platoons. His son, First Lieutenant Tyus, our second in command, stood next to his father.

"Boys, welcome to Company F. We are one of eleven companies that comprise the Texas Fifteenth Regiment of Cavalry under Colonel George H. Sweet. We will train briefly here at Personville before we join the other companies in the regiment. For now, we're assigned to the Trans-Mississippi District and could see duty west of the Mississippi River. That could change in the twinkling of an eye. First you'll learn how to function together as platoons and a company. Then we'll join the other companies to learn regimental maneuvers. If you need anything, go to your corporal. If he can't help you, go to your sergeant. If that doesn't work, then seek out your lieutenant. Failing that, you may address your issues with me, but only after you have followed the chain of command. God bless all of you. God bless Texas. Company dismissed."

———————

First and Second Squads comprised First Platoon under Lieutenant Kinney. First Squad was under Sergeant Howard and Corporals Ham Howard and Joseph Riley. Riley was quick as a cat with blond hair and blue eyes like his brothers, who were also in our squad, John and Wade Riley. There was a whole family of relatives in our squad. There was the father, Bryan Wade, who was the company's assistant surgeon. While he tended the whole company, he ate and camped with our platoon. He had two sons, T. J., the older, and Jake, the younger. T.J. was serious about everything; Jake wasn't serious about anything. He was our company clown and kept things cheered up when he could, although he sometimes got some stern remarks from his father or the lieutenant. Their cousin, Pecos Wade, was the farrier. His job was to tend the horses' feet and help the blacksmith. His older brother, Buddy, was in our squad, as was their good friend,

John Stone, the blacksmith. John didn't have a lot to say, but when he did, it was worth listening to.

Second Squad was under Sergeant Barnett, whose son, Ethan, served in the same squad. He was assisted by Corporal Harold Payton, whose little brother, Bradley, was with him. They were as different as night and day. Harold was about six feet tall, dark complexioned, with black hair and dark eyes. Bradley, was five years younger, slightly built, not too tall, with blond hair and blue eyes. You would have never known they were brothers if they hadn't told it.

The other corporal in Second Squad was Clint Hunter. Clint was a man of near middle age, with a quick wit and smile. He had five sons serving with him. Joshua was the oldest and strongest; then followed Jonathan, Jordan, Justin and Jamison, in descending age. They were a lot of fun and had plenty of musical talent. They all liked to sing and dance, and had brought musical instruments with them. Second Squad was rounded out with brothers Will and Calvin Anderson, Joseph Evans, Monty McNeal, and Dane Carthel. Lieutenant Kinney expected us to know the name of every man in the platoon, plus his hometown, before we joined up into the regiment. He explained that we would be depending on each other for our lives. He already knew every single one of us.

All these names, all these faces would become a part of my memory for the rest of my life. Although no one would ever take the place of Noah, David or Pink, these men would become like my own family. The heat of battle and the hammer of war would shape us and change us until we became as one. Those early days, so golden at the time, would darken and tarnish with time and bloodstains, but their memories would never leave me. As for now, I was on a great adventure with my new friends and my family as we set out upon the road to glory.

4

March 1862, Regimental Headquarters,
near Greenville, Texas

COMPANY F BROKE CAMP
and rode northeast toward the lush black land prairie
east of Greenville. Our travelling company consisted of
more than one hundred and twenty mounted men and
officers, a military ambulance and three heavily loaded
supply wagons. The freight wagons were each pulled by
four good quality mules, and the ambulance was drawn
by a pair of solid light draft horses. At the head of our
little column, Trent Kinney had been given the honor of
carrying our company colors. Our flag was the "Bonnie
Blue" flag of solid dark blue with a large single white star
in the center. Embroidered under the star with heavy gold
thread were stitched the words Texas Fifteenth Cavalry,
Company F. The weather was crisp and cool. We wore
our capes over our waistcoats. They fluttered joyously in
the light breeze. I rode next to Lieutenant Kinney ready
to carry a message to anyone, someone. It was an exciting
time for a twelve year old boy to be alive.

All along the way there, from isolated cabins to
small towns, people came out to the road to cheer for us.
Our camps along the way were filled with laughter and
stories. The Hunter family broke out their guitars, fiddles,

and an Irish flute to play for us, while one or the other of them beat out the time on the upturned end of a wooden crate. They danced hornpipes and jigs and something called Irish step dancing. It was a sight to see and kept us entertained. A farmer north of Waco had butchered a pair of longhorn steers. He had spent all day cooking them in our honor, with kettles of beans, pans of cornbread and countless pots of coffee. After supper, several jugs of corn liquor circulated through camp. Noah and I partook of our share whenever David wasn't watching. We wanted him to keep thinking we had never tasted the stuff. But we knew where Lige Campbell had kept some of his jugs hidden. Had he been a more careful man, he might have noticed it was a little watered down sometimes.

In a week, we were camped outside Greenville with the other ten companies of the Texas Fifteenth Regiment of Cavalry. The regimental camp spread out across the native prairie in row upon row of orderly tents. Hundreds and hundreds of horses and mules were picketed in long rows. There were more people here than I ever remembered seeing in one place. And since headquarters was here, I actually got to carry dispatches along the straight streets of our tent city. Captain Tyus had commented that there were over fifteen hundred men in the camp and nearly two thousand horses and mules. There was a regimental bakery that made real bread, fresh every morning. There was a regimental hospital tent overflowing with surgeons and orderlies. Each company flew its own flag, but our own Bonnie Blue flag was the prettiest to me. The Confederate Stars and Bars flew at Headquarters. The solid blue field with a circle of seven stars was joined by broad horizontal bands of red and white. It was a beautiful flag. But in my inner thoughts, I felt it strange that the Stars and Stripes were absent. I dared not share those thoughts aloud. It had not really soaked into my brain yet that Texas was no longer a part of the United States.

We practiced regimental maneuvers until the men and horses

could do them in their sleep. Seeing a thousand mounted men wheel, turn and charge in another direction was amazing. The thundering of the hooves pounding the black prairie soil shook the ground. When the whole unit charged full out raising the Rebel yell, it gave me goose bumps. The sound that rose from a thousand throats was hard to describe. It was a yipping sound, kind of like coyotes hunting for a rabbit. It rose in pitch and volume until it ended in a prolonged blood curdling wail. That sound was etched into my memory for the rest of my life. I usually had to stay with the officers for messages, but sometimes Captain Tyus would let me join in with the others, under Sergeant Howard's watchful eye.

As a messenger, I got to see the officers up close and personal. Some of them had gorgeous expensive uniforms. Colonel Sweet wore a red ostrich plume in his hat and a red silk sash around his waist. Some of the lieutenant colonels and majors were dressed in similar fashion. But I was still proud of my homemade uniform. There were actually dispatches for me to gallop across the fields. I felt like I was doing something important and glorious. My head was so swollen with pride that my cap barely fit. Life was grand on the road to glory.

I raced Wichita directly to Captain Tyus. My heart was pounding with excitement. "Captain Tyus, sir? With Colonel Sweet's compliments, sir."

He grinned at my eagerness. "Yes, Private Turner? Have the Yankees crossed the Red River?"

"Oh, no sir. I've got a written dispatch for you, sir!" I remembered that the canvas envelope was still inside my leather pouch. "Oh, I beg your pardon, sir." As it was the only dispatch in the pouch, it wasn't too hard to find. My cheeks were red with excitement and embarrassment as I handed it to him.

He pulled his reading glasses out of his coat pocket. "Well, Private Turner, it's not a secret any more. The whole regiment will leave in the morning to reinforce Fort Hindman on the Arkansas River in southern Arkansas. I am required to sign an acknowledgement of receipt of this order. You are to take it to each platoon in the company." He neatly signed the order, handing it back to me. "Well what are you waiting for Aaron? Ride, son, ride!" As similar news spread throughout the huge encampment, cheering echoed from every direction. No more practice and drill. This was real. We were riding off to war.

The next morning, well before daylight, we began to pull our things together for the road. We were ready to travel. The regimental officers and their staff took the point position, and each company, A through K, followed in turn. Each company was to maintain about two hundred yards road distance to keep the dust down. The entire Fifteenth Regiment strung out almost two miles. But by the second day, the dust was not our problem. It started to rain. At first, it was just a spring shower, but as the day progressed, the rain came heavier and heavier until it fell in unending sheets of soaking rain. The rain turned the Texarkana Road into a slippery, slimy black mess. This was not ordinary soil under our feet; it was a thing of legend: east Texas "Black Gumbo." The good quality mules pulling the wagons handled it well enough, but the extra burden of the clinging black mud on each wheel tired them quickly. We made a hard twenty miles the first day of the mud.

The camp was situated on high ground that shed the still falling rain. We got the tents set up in spite of the rain. We dug shallow trenches around them to divert the run-off away from the tents. The rain made it impossible to cook a hot supper, so we contented ourselves with hard tack and jerky.

The next day's journey on the Dallas to Texarkana Road, the soil changed from black to grayish red. It was still sticky, but better than the gumbo. The animals suffered less in the lighter mud, although we all had to endure the continuing cold spring rain. Another miserable day passed. The road became sandy, packed by the rain and our travel over it. We made twenty-five miles and camped on a ridge near Sulphur Springs with good grass and some scattered timber. The skies were still gray, but clearing enough that we could have a hot supper. It sure tasted good, especially the hot coffee.

In four days, we were at the ford on the Red River. The muddy water turned south to form the border between Texas and Arkansas before it flowed across Louisiana and merged into the mighty Mississippi. The river bed was firm enough to ford and shallow enough for the wagons to cross. Once the column had cleared the bottom land along the river, we camped on a sandy ridge of pine trees and grass in the southwest corner of Arkansas. It was the first time I had travelled outside of Texas. David and Pink had both been to Natchitoches, Louisiana, and Pink had once even been to New Orleans, but for Noah and me, this was high adventure.

As we bedded down for the night in our tent, we heard a blood curdling scream from Brandon Moss. There was something alive inside his bedroll. When he shook it out, a large bullfrog blinked at us then hopped away. We were all laughing pretty hard, but from the way Taylor Edwards laughed, I suspected he and the frog had met previously.

The regiment continued across southern Arkansas until we were on the southwest bank of the mighty Arkansas River. It was a mile wide, swift and deep. The river banks were high, steep, clay bluffs. There was no ford for many miles in any direction. The imposing earthen walls of Fort Hindman stared down in an ugly threat from it heights above the river. Cannon protruded from bastions around the fort. The road to glory had led us to a mud fort in the middle of a swamp.

5

May, 1862, Fort Hindman, southeast Arkansas

WE HAD TO CAMP ONE
night on the wrong side of the river. The mosquitoes
swarmed in choking buzzing clouds. We had brought
pouches of what we called "Chance's Miracle Mosquito
Salve." It was made from rancid animal fat, roots, and
herbs. It smelled horrible, but it kept the mosquitoes
away. We shared with the men in our platoon.

The next day, Colonel Sweet appeared angry after
opening an order from Arkansas General Churchill. The
entire regiment was to be dismounted. The Confederacy
needed the horses east of the Mississippi. Only officers
and messengers were to keep their mounts. He wrote
explicit orders to all company commanders. I carried
the dreadful orders to each company. They were to be
signed and acknowledged. The company captains were
all angry, very angry. Captain Tyus' blue eyes flashed
lightning.

"By thunder, Private, I don't like this! I didn't ride
across all of hell and half of Texas to come to a swamp in
Arkansas and have some bureaucrat in Richmond turnin'
my fine cavalry into foot soldiers!"

I only saluted and continued my rounds. What could I say? He was right. The Confederacy was going to give $50 in script for each horse and $10 for each saddle. The grumbling among the men rose to a fevered pitch. Some of the men said they would just take their horses and go home.

Colonel Sweet came to each of the eleven companies in the Fifteenth Regiment and made about the same speech to each one. "Men of Texas, our lives, our families, our homes, our very way of life, have been threatened by the aggressive behavior of the northern states. When the Indians threatened, we banded together and fought them. When the Mexicans threatened Texas, we came together as a nation and fought them. Now we are threatened again. We have unified ourselves in common cause to drive the Yankees from the South and leave us in peace. I expected to fight from the back of a fine horse. The South says my horse, and all of yours, are needed elsewhere. We have offered our lives in defense of the South. Are we to withhold the use of our horses? We will fight the Yankees on foot. Our bullets will kill them just as dead. You men all signed an oath to support and defend the Confederacy. A man who won't stand by his oath is no son of Texas. I am counting on all of you to do your duty. Any of you who have other ideas are traitors to Texas and will be treated as deserters!"

The next morning, we found that about fifty men had taken their horses and left, including one man I didn't know from another platoon in our company. All day long, two ferries steamed the regiment across the Arkansas, leaving their horses behind. The high imposing banks of the river only added to the somber mood of the now dismounted regiment. A dark cloud of dissatisfaction and unhappiness settled over all of us.

Once we had all been transported across the river, we spent the next few days setting up our camp. The hulking gloom of the fort was to the south of us. The Arkansas angled from northwest to southeast, an impossible barrier. Behind us, closing the triangle of misery was a cypress swamp. Its stagnant water was interspersed with ridges or islands of slightly higher ground covered with great stands of mixed hardwoods, live oaks, white oaks, elms, and magnolia. They were sprinkled with stands of pines. Between these islands, the swamp was filled with cypress trees covered with shrouds of Spanish moss.

The evening mists rolled out of the swamp each night to smother our camp with a damp blanket of fog and mosquitoes. Noah and I got the idea of making and selling the mosquito salve. We kept some ripening all the time with unusable parts of slaughtered army cattle and plants we collected in the swamp. We sewed leather pouches from pieces of green cowhide and filled them with the salve. We couldn't keep up with the demand. It brought five cents with the pouch or two cents for a refill. It was one of the only things for which the soldiers would part with a scrap of hard money.

As I carried a report to Captain Tyus he gave me an odd look. "Private Turner, you smell like a dead skunk. Have you given up bathing?"

"Beggin' the Captain's pardon, sir, I bathe regular, and put on clean drawers. I put on 'Chance's Miracle Mosquito Salve' to keep the skeeters off."

As he swatted swarming pests away from his face he asked "Does it work, son?"

"Like a charm, sir. Seein' as you're my commandin' officer, let me give ya a pouch to try."

The next time I saw the captain, he caught me by the arm. "By thunder, Aaron, that vile smellin' stuff works just like you said. I want a steady supply until the dead of winter. Count me as a payin' customer."

—————

The regiment was put to using picks and spades digging trenches and rifle pits to protect the approaches to the fort from the southeast. We all complained about the work on a daily basis. Summer in the swamps of southeastern Arkansas was more miserable than a man could imagine.

We each received a letter from home. Momma said things were good. They had planted mostly corn, just a little cotton, tobacco, beans and peas. The cotton took lots of labor, and the extra food crops would be easy to sell with a war in progress. David's letter from Alma indicated he had done a little 'planting,' too, before he left home. Alma was expecting a baby.

Summer turned into fall without much excitement. The huge guns at Fort Hindman discouraged any Union shipping from trying to travel up the Arkansas. Lieutenant Kinney released Noah and me to hunt and scavenge. Hogs ran wild in the swamps, feeding on acorns. Several times we shot some that we dressed and brought to camp. We always shared some of the best cuts with Captain Tyus, before we parceled it out with the platoon, then the rest of the company if there was enough to go around. We sometimes brought back deer and turkey. Sergeant Howard and his family ran fishing lines in the river with the help of a small rowboat they "borrowed" somewhere. The catfish were big and good eating.

Noah and I caught a plate sized snapping turtle in the edge of the swamp that had a real nasty attitude. We hauled him back to camp in a tow sack, popping his jaws the whole way. We kind of suggested to Brandon Moss that maybe Taylor Edwards might need some company in his bedroll. He quickly agreed and slid the fractious snapper under Taylor's blankets just before "Taps" sounded that night.

"Aaagh! There's somethin' in my bed! It's got me by my little toe! Ahhh! It's bitin' my toe! Git it off! Git it off!" He had jumped out of the bed, screaming, trying to get the turtle off. A quickly lighted candle revealed the snapper had a tight hold of Taylor's little toe and a wad of sock. Poor Taylor was screaming like he was being skinned alive by a Comanche.

I assessed the situation. "Taylor, there ain't nothin' we can do but chop off his head with this here axe. Noah, you hold him real still while I do the whackin'."

"Ahhh, get away from me. Y'all are crazy! You're gonna cut off my whole foot!" He kicked with all his might. The turtle flew across the tent with Taylor's sock and a little piece of his toe in its mouth. Pink threw the turtle in the river and we all laughed until our sides hurt. Taylor recovered nicely.

———————

By late December, fun and games were over. A lone Union ironclad was spotted slowly making its way against the current toward the fort. It was a squat ugly thing. It was pointed at both ends, rather narrow, with a single revolving turret on top displaying a single huge gun. It seemed to be in no hurry. Black coal smoke curled out of a smoke stack that barely cleared the low deck. What it lacked it beauty it made up in sheer deadliness, like a large alligator swimming slowly in the water: ugly, but ready to kill instantly.

As it rounded the bend in the river just below the fort it came into range of the fort's great guns. Fort Hindman's guns came alive. One heavy shell splashed very near the ironclad. The next hit it with a great clang and ricocheted off like a pebble hitting a brick wall. It crawled relentlessly closer to the fort. The iron turret turned slowly until it was in line with the fort, its lone great gun elevated to the maximum. A huge orange fireball preceded the loudest blast I had ever heard. There was a deep thud followed a split second later by an explosion that caused an entire earthen section of the fort's wall to heave up into the air before collapsing into a shapeless pile of dirt. The gunboat allowed its bow to swing downstream and it slowly disappeared around the bend. The gunners in the fort were too shocked to even return fire. We all knew we were in serious trouble.

6

January 1863, Fort Hindman, Arkansas Post, Arkansas

ON JANUARY 9, 1863, A messenger galloped to Fort Hindman on a lathered horse with an urgent dispatch for General Churchill. Yankee infantry were landing in large force at Notrebe's Plantation on the northeast bank of the Arkansas, the same side on which the fort stood. Moments later, another courier raced to headquarters. A division of Union troops was moving up the opposite bank of the river hauling a large number of huge cannon. As if things could not get worse, a third rider arrived on an exhausted horse. A whole fleet of Union gunboats were heading up the Arkansas led by three ironclads.

Word came to Colonel Sweet to be ready to defend the trenches protecting the western approaches to the fort. He sent me with a verbal order to every company in the regiment to prepare for immediate action. The huge guns of the fort could hold back the troops approaching from the southeast. They could handle the Union gunboats, but not the three ironclads. Troops couldn't easily scale the twenty-five foot bluffs of the Arkansas. We had trenches covering that whole approach if the Yankees decided to try it. But the image of the shell bouncing harmlessly off the ironclad Union gunboat was seared into my memory.

The troops holding the trenches southeast of the fort came flooding back to take up new positions. They had retreated in the presence of no less than thirty thousand Union infantry! Our entire force was only about five thousand counting bakers and musicians. The east facing guns of the fort opened fire on the cautiously approaching Union force. The blue uniforms now filled the trenches so recently occupied by our soldiers that hot Confederate meals awaited the Yankees in still simmering pots.

"Noah, reckon why they stopped?"

"I don't know. Maybe they're scared of those big guns on the fort. I know I would be."

The morning air was shattered by a thunderous blast and a loud whistling sound. The ground shook beneath our feet. There was a deep thud, followed by an enormous explosion. The Yankee gunships had arrived, led by the three ironclads. The initial shot was followed by a near continuous bombardment of one hundred pound exploding shells.

The gunboats targeted each of the fort's guns. The gunners in the fort could only fire at the three ironclad ships as the others were protected by the bend in the river. They could fire at the fort, but the big guns of Fort Hindman couldn't touch them. Colored flags from the Union forces in the trenches near the fort indicated they had artillery spotters signaling adjustments to the gunboats. The return fire from the fort began to sputter and then stopped as the last gun was disabled. The Union shelling continued until the once menacing Fort Hindman was nothing more than a smoldering, pockmarked mound of dirt. The garrison soldiers joined us in the trenches behind the ruins of the fort. Nightfall brought an eerie, ominous silence to the battlefield.

Through the still night air we could hear troop movements across the river. We would catch a word or two of a shouted order, the jangle of trace chains on draft horses, and the calls of teamsters to their mules. Torches and campfires soon sparkled in the cold clear night from the bluffs across the Arkansas.

The swamps wrapped around us in a crescent on two sides to the north and west. Thirty thousand Yankees stood between the edge of the swamp and the bank of the river to the southeast. In our front, the impassable Arkansas River was filled with warships and the far bank lined with troops and cannon. We were in a box from which there was no way out.

In the purple light of the false dawn, a tremendous salvo shook the earth as seventeen Union gunboats fired in unison from beneath the shelter of the opposite bluff of the Arkansas. Anyone or anything standing above and behind the shelter of our trenches was blown to bits by the exploding shells. I looked back to see my horse, Wichita, turned into an unrecognizable mass of gore. I vomited in the trench. A second volley from the big guns fell just short of the trenches, blowing gaping craters in the soft ground.

"They've got us in range now, boys! Git down! Git down!" Sergeant Howard shouted.

The third salvo hit squarely against the earth and log breast works across the front of our trenches. Men pulled their friends from the shattered earth and splintered logs. Mercifully, a fourth volley wasn't fired. The gunboats fell silent. In the ominous silence in the fog along the river, the sound of thousands of troops falling into position echoed through the gloom. Bugles, hundreds of bugles, sounded along the river. Thirty thousand Yankees surged over the torn ground toward the remnants of our defenses. The large shell craters slowed them long enough for our officers to get us into some kind of order to mount a defense. The blue clad soldiers swarmed out of the fog at only a hundred feet away.

Company F was near the center of the destroyed line where the heaviest attack came. I lay on the disturbed ground with an elm log above my head with Noah, David and Pink. We all fired and reloaded as fast as we could. The blue uniforms were so thick, I just shot without picking a target.

The attackers retreated, regrouped, and pressed in again. The thin gray line held, but just barely. This time the Union troops left the field and disappeared behind the remnants of the fort. A faint cheer went up as some of the boys thought we had driven them off. But as the fog lifted and thin sunlight filtered down, we saw why they had moved away. A Yankee battery of over fifty heavy guns glared at us from the bluff across the river. A single volley tore through our lines. We knew we were doomed. First one, and then another, white shirt began to appear from our ruined defenses. The Battle of Fort Hindman was over. The mighty Arkansas River lay open to the Union forces all the way to Little Rock.

7

January, 1863, Mississippi River, somewhere between Arkansas and Tennessee

THE SURRENDER HAD BEEN less terrifying than I had expected. We had walked out of the trenches with our arms held high while Yankee soldiers removed any weapons or war materials we had. We were allowed to retrieve our bedrolls and war bags. When they had searched everything carefully, they had returned our things to us. They didn't take our money, personal belongings or even the little bits of food we had with us. The horde of coins Noah and I had amassed was dumped from the two socks that held our treasure, then handed back to us. Our officers had called a company muster. Two men from Company F were missing; either hiding in the swamp or dead in the debris of the trenches. Our assistant surgeon, Bryan Wade, had been killed as was one other man I did not know. The Yankees allowed us to bury them there. The regimental surgeons had tended our wounded. Corporal Riley had a broken jaw from a piece of log smashing him in the face. Dane Carthel had a broken ankle. The surgeons set it and said it should heal.

Once we had been checked off the company roster, we were loaded on steam transports destined for prison camp. The officers were loaded on a separate steamer. It would take them to Camp Chase, Ohio. Trent Kinney was sent with his father. Captain Tyus explained to us that Union General McClernand, who had commanded the Federal troops at Fort Hindman, had told him that prisoner exchanges were occurring regularly. It was likely we would be exchanged in a few weeks or months. The enlisted men were being sent to Camp Stephen Douglas in Chicago.

"Davey, I've heard that name somewhere."

"Yep, he's the man that ran for President for the Northern Union Party in 1860; he came in second behind Lincoln."

We were tightly packed on the transports but humanely treated. We had one hot meal a day, and two meals of hard tack and coffee. When I could, I climbed up as high as they would let me go on the steamer and watched the countryside roll past. In places, all I could see were sweeping bluffs, but in others, I could see mile after mile of good farmland lying fallow for the winter to end and the spring planting to begin. Some of the land was planted to winter grains like wheat, oats or barley. It was green and beautiful. Seeing the farmland made me homesick for our place on the Navasota River, for Momma, for hunting in the forests with my brothers. All of those things seemed so long ago and far away. I had only been gone less than a year, but it already seemed like a lifetime.

At Cairo, Illinois, the Ohio River joins the Mississippi. The confluence of the rivers made for rough water and shifting sandbars. The steamboat captain had men out on the front of the boat casting weighted lines to watch the depth for shoals. It was here the steamer carrying our officers broke off to journey on alone up the Ohio. Their steamer blasted a shrill farewell as the officers lined the rails and waved to the other boats. Our transport returned the salute with its brass steam whistle as we crowded the rails to wave goodbye.

We travelled up the Mississippi with Illinois to our right and Missouri on our left until we came to the confluence of the Illinois River. Here we left the Mississippi and began to steam across the heart of Illinois. Small and large farms lined the river on both sides. The land looked fertile and prosperous. As we travelled further northeast, we began to see factories of every imaginable type lining the river, their great smoke stacks reaching the clouds.

Finally, we reached our destination in Chicago. We were mustered off the transports by our sergeants, and kept together by platoons. We marched through Chicago's muddy streets. Somehow I had expected the whole city to be made of gold. It was not. It was just another town, although larger than others I had seen. A few loafers threw snowballs and rocks at us, but our Yankee guards drove them away.

Camp Stephen Douglas was located on eighty acres of swampy land on the far side of Chicago. Perhaps it was the gray winter skies and drizzle that made it look so forlorn, but it was a place of gloomy unhappiness. We marched past relatively neat officers' quarters, guards' barracks and a bakery. Gray clad prisoners with ankle chains sloshed from one chore to another outside the gates. When we reached the tall wooden palisades that enclosed the camp, a heavy guard detail met us outside and another was waiting inside the gates.

The interior of those walls enclosed a place of misery. Row upon row of mildewing canvas tents lined streets of mud. A small stream meandered through the camp trying vainly to carry away the filth of thousands of men. Wooden latrines lined the ruined stream.

We finally stopped at a vacant six-man tent. Ten of us were detailed to stay here. The occupants were to be Sergeant Howard, his three sons and two nephews, Noah, David, Pink and me. The tent had a filthy wooden floor and nothing else. There were no cots, no blankets, and no stove. The bedrolls we had brought with us from our capture in Arkansas would have to do. Sergeant Howard looked around with resignation in his voice. "Well, boys, it's a long way from Texas, and a long time 'til spring."

We fell into the routine of the camp quickly. We proceeded by company to the mess tent for our meals. Our breakfast consisted of a bowl of oatmeal or cornmeal mush. There was no coffee, just hot water to drink. Lunch was one potato boiled in the jacket without salt. Supper was bean or peas with a very little bit of salt pork chopped up into it. We had to use our own bowls and utensils. There was a large wash tub of hot water in which to rinse our dishes. By the end of the line, it was hardly worth the trouble.

Every morning before breakfast there was a roll call of each company by platoon. Within a few days, more names were added to the sick list each morning. In two weeks, the first names were tolled off as dead.

The camp had stinking latrines lining the creek, but nowhere to bathe. We were allowed to bring buckets of hot water on Sundays from the mess hall to our tents in an effort to stay clean. I was glad to have the lye soap Mother had sent with me. I used a sock as a wash rag and got as clean as I could. Once those who had wanted to wash up were finished, we used the left over water to rinse out our clothes. No one would accuse them of being clean, but they were less filthy than they were.

We were detailed different jobs around the camp. Noah and I were assigned to the hospital as orderlies. Some of the others worked in the mess tent or bakery. Those who had aggravated the guards found themselves scrubbing out the latrines. It seemed Jake Wade and Taylor Edwards often had that job.

In the hospital, the Yankee doctors came twice a day to the ward to make a quick check of the patients. It was one of our jobs to point out patients that needed extra attention. We were required to help the doctors at surgery. Sometimes they would have to remove a bullet from an old wound or amputate an arm or leg that had developed gangrene. We didn't particularly like that part of our job, but I kept my eyes and ears open and tried to learn everything I could. I listened when the doctors made their rounds and discussed the patients with dysentery or pneumonia. Sometimes I would ask the doctors questions. They got to the point if they had something interesting, they would take the time to show me. They taught me how to do simple wound care, lance a boil and how to close cuts with crude sutures. They would leave anatomy and medical books for me to read in the hospital tent, if I had extra time. Noah was less interested, but encouraged me to learn more. There was little they could do for many of their patients. They could keep them clean and well-fed, but not much else. If they needed a limb removed, the doctors had sufficient skills that most of their patients survived. They used ether to keep them asleep during surgery.

We wrote letters for the sick and injured soldiers to their family and loved ones who were not able to do it for themselves. Some could read and write, some could not; but all were too sick. We read any letters they received to them, but those were rare, and we often read favorite passages to them from the Bible and gave comfort where we could. We were allowed to return to the hospital after supper at night until "Taps" sounded. As the men died, it was our job to record their names and units with a copy going to their platoon sergeant. We returned their blankets and war bags so that the men in their platoon could use what few possessions they had.

Two Chicago boys worked with us as orderlies in the hospital, Johnny and Brian Schwartz. They were about our ages and we gradually became friends with them. Their father had been killed early in the war. They were from a large family and were working to try to help their mother keep body and soul together. It sounded like their life in Chicago wasn't much easier than ours in the camp. They were always on the alert for useful things that were being wasted or unsupervised. Often the officers' mess would have left over food. They were given all they wanted. They would take what they could carry home in tow sacks. If there was more than they could use, they gave it to us. Sometimes it would be a few boiled potatoes, or part of bread loaves, but sometimes there would be a little left over meat of some kind. Our tent mates were glad for anything extra we brought to them.

———

One after the other, each of us in the tent and the whole camp, became ill with body aches, high fever, and cough. We all were excused from our assigned duties. Those healthy enough to go to the mess tent were allowed to carry food back to their ill tent mates. Sergeant Howard said it was "the grippe." Whatever it was, it made us miserable.

David was the last one in our tent to come down with it. His fever lasted about three days and seemed to be getting gradually better. A week later, his face had a gray cast to it. The fever came roaring back with pain in his chest and a deep cough. Noah and I had seen plenty of pneumonia and knew this was what he had. He refused to go to the hospital because nobody ever came out alive. Finally, he was so weak that Pink and Skeet carried him to the hospital.

The doctors confirmed that he had pneumonia. They allowed us to make him as comfortable as possible. Johnny and Brian brought the leftovers of a chicken from the officers' mess. They made a broth out of it with a few flecks of chicken meat. David was too weak to eat it. We set him up and spoon fed him half a cup of broth. We bathed him as well as we could, washed his clothes, and redressed him when they were dry.

We both stayed at his bedside all night long. His fever was so high he talked out of his head. He talked to Alma, Momma, even to Father. Come daylight he seemed a little better. He drank a whole cup of broth. He asked for a pencil and paper to write letters to Momma and Alma. He was too weak, so we wrote what he said.

> Dear Alma, Mother, and Mary Ann,
> I hope this letter finds you well. As you may have heard, we were captured at Fort Hindman, Arkansas. We have been in a prison camp in Chicago for about a month. The camp is not very comfortable and the food is not very good, but the guards treat us fairly. Noah, Aaron, and Pink are all doing fine. I have fallen ill and am having

the boys write this for me. Please know I love each of you very much and long for the day when I shall see you again.

> Love,
> David
> Private, Fifteenth Texas Cavalry, Dismounted,
> Company F

David seemed to want to talk that afternoon. He told us stories about our family, things that he had been told, and things that he remembered. He told us as much as he could remember of Father and Father's family in South Carolina. He finally said he was tired and wanted to rest. We sat at his bedside and watched him sleep.

Before the doctors came back to make their afternoon rounds, David took a deep breath and sighed. He opened his eyes and reached out a hand. "I'm coming." He closed his eyes and slumped back into his pillow. He was gone. We felt his chest and confirmed his heart had stopped beating. We sat, each holding a slowly cooling hand, as tears rolled down our cheeks. When the doctors came, they added his name to the dead list. Johnny and Brian carried him away.

They told us later that he had been buried in a trench grave on Confederate Mound in Oak Ridge Cemetery near Chicago. They made sure his name was on the burial list. Buddy Wade and Lath Howard died before the end of February, both with pneumonia.

David had been our link to our father. With his death, Noah and I felt like orphans. Pink did a good job of stepping up to take care of us. But we always knew that with David's death we had lost a part of ourselves.

———

In March, word came that we were to be exchanged. We were mustered out of the camp by platoons and companies. We gathered our few tattered belongings and rolled them in our bedrolls which we tied across our chests. We were marched back through Chicago and loaded on transport steamers. I was glad to be leaving the camp, very glad. But I had left part of my heart there with David.

We steamed down the Illinois River, seeing the coming of spring. We entered the Mississippi River and descended the Father of Waters to Cairo. There we ascended the Ohio River. A few days upriver, we saw another steamer put off from shore and make all speed to pass the line of transports. As they passed, the newly joined steamer blasted a continuous greeting on its steam whistle. Lining the decks were our officers. On the top deck we spotted Captain Tyus, Lieutenant Kinney and Trent waving hard to us as they passed. The officers' steamer assumed its place at the head of the procession. It seemed as if the world was starting to get back in its right order.

The country on either bank of the Ohio was beautiful. The forest was breaking out in early light green buds. Mixed among them were redbuds, dogwoods and wild fruit trees. The farms were far advanced with their spring preparations. The farm houses and barns were tidy and neatly painted. Well tended fruit orchards were in full bloom. Small dairies dotted the fertile countryside. The countryside spoke of a quiet prosperity. As we approached the larger cities, factories appeared up and down the valley of the Ohio. The farther we went upriver, the greater the concentration of factories. The industrial might of the North was evident among the smokestacks. As I saw these things, I began to wonder if the South was like a jay bird fighting an eagle.

We reached Wheeling, in what was now known as West Virginia. The Stars and Stripes flew there. We were ordered off the transports and reunited with our officers. Captain Tyus looked thin and gaunt, as did Lieutenant Kinney and Trent. They greeted us warmly. First Lieutenant Tyus, the Captain's son, had died of a fever in Ohio. Colonel Sweet had been replaced. A Colonel Deshler would assume command once we had been exchanged. There was a festive mood on the docks at Wheeling.

Without wasting any time, we were loaded into boxcars with fresh straw on the floor. The cars were pulled by engines of the

Baltimore and Ohio Railroad. Each boxcar had barrels of fresh water, hard tack, and jerky. There were slop buckets for our use in curtained corners. There were no guards in the boxcars, but there were two passenger cars full of armed guards and a boxcar full of supplies. There were also two platform cars of saddled Union cavalry mounts. Their riders filled the adjacent boxcar ready to pursue any prisoners foolish enough to try to escape. Each time the train stopped for coal or water, some of our men were detailed to refill the water barrel, pick up more rations, and empty the slop buckets.

In a day and a half our boxcars were transferred to engines from the Baltimore and Chesapeake Railroad for our trip down the peninsula of Virginia to Fortress Monroe. At the outbreak of the war, the Union had recognized the strategic importance this fort held. It commanded the approaches to Chesapeake Bay, the James and the Potomac Rivers. They had rushed reinforcements there, and it had stood firmly in Union hands ever since. It was here the exchange was to take place.

Sometime the next day, prisoners held by the Confederacy reached a predetermined location near the fort. Once the Yankee soldiers were safely in Union hands, we were released to Confederate agents. Colonel Deshler was there to meet us and assume command of the regiment. We boarded boxcars on the Richmond and Chesapeake Railroad for the few hours to Richmond. There we were taken to a huge camp on the rolling hills of Virginia near the capital.

The tents stood in clean neat rows like a huge city. There were bakery, mess, and hospital tents. There were sanitary latrines and tents set up for bathing, complete with hot water, soap and towels. The food was good and included fresh vegetables, a little fruit, and meat. We got coffee once a day. The medical officers and dentists evaluated each of us for fitness to return to duty. Our regimental structure quickly reasserted itself. We were rearmed, reclothed, and fully re-equipped.

During the summer of 1863, while we reorganized at Richmond, great events shaped the war. General Lee with the Army of Northern Virginia had invaded deep into Pennsylvania. His invasion had created panic in the North and created chaos in Washington. The Northern Peace Party pushed for a negotiated settlement with the South. Great Britain and France watched with great interest. A Southern victory here might bring much needed diplomatic recognition of the Confederacy. The United States had been at war with Great Britain only thirty-eight years ago, and there was no love lost between them now. In the event they entered the war on the side of the Confederacy, the Union was doomed. All eyes were turned on Gettysburg, Pennsylvania, on July 3. After a hard fought battle, with tremendous loss of life on both sides, the forces under Lee suffered a great defeat. The diplomatic hopes of the South were dashed.

The western half of the Confederacy consisted of Arkansas, Louisiana, the Indian Nations, the Territories of Arizona and New Mexico, and Texas, the great source of men, beef, cotton and corn. All these men and materials flowed from their respective states to the Red River at Natchitoches, Louisiana. From there they moved down the Red River to the section of the Mississippi still in Confederate hands between Port Hudson and Vicksburg. This link was vital to the continued movement of much needed reinforcements and war goods to the rest of the South.

On July 4, 1863, the siege of Vicksburg ended with the fall of that great city. Days later, Port Hudson fell to the Union. Yankee shipping flowed unimpeded down the Mississippi from its source far to the north to the Gulf of Mexico. The Confederacy was cut in half. The last remaining link to Texas was severed. Now, there was no way home. At Gettysburg, the hope of the Confederacy for victory had died. At Vicksburg, the hope of the South for survival had perished.

8

September, 1863, southeastern Tennessee

I WAS THIRTEEN NOW, pushing six feet tall, mostly arms and legs. Noah was fifteen. He had finally topped out at six foot three inches. We had ridden the Richmond and Chattanooga Railroad to the hills of southeastern Tennessee. Our regiment, the Texas Fifteenth Cavalry, Dismounted, was usually just called the Texas Fifteenth. It was commanded by Colonel Deshler. Because of our notorious surrender in Arkansas, several divisional commanders declined to have our regiment assigned to their unit. We had been boxed into a corner at Fort Hindman. We were outnumbered thirty thousand to five thousand. We had faced a whole flotilla of Union gunboats, and another division of infantry with fifty heavy guns raking us across the river. But the "cat calls" persisted.

General Patrick Cleburne had been born in Ireland and eventually immigrated to Texas. He had red hair, blue eyes, and a thick Irish accent. He was known as one of the toughest, hardest fighting divisional commanders in the Army of Tennessee. He looked over our division and decided we hadn't been given a fair test in battle. He personally requested that the Texas Fifteenth Regiment be added to his Division. It was a fateful decision. The Fifteenth would flourish under Cleburne into one of the top units in the Army, and the Fifteenth came to love Pat Cleburne to the point they would lay down their lives for him.

A letter reached us from Momma. It looked like it had been to China and back. It must have crossed the Mississippi before Vicksburg had fallen.

Dear David, Noah, Aaron and Pinckney,

I have mixed news for you boys. David, Alma gave birth to a beautiful baby girl we named Alice in January. Sadly, there were complications. Alma died a few days later. We buried her here with the family. The baby is fine. David, I am so sorry for you. I will raise Alice as my own until you return. Pink, Mary Ann is well and sends her love. Noah and Aaron, I so wish to see you and know you are well. We are getting by here at home well enough. I pray for each of you every night.

Love,
Mother

"Noah, Momma must not have gotten the letter about David. This had to have been sent before he died. That baby Alice ain't got a mother or father. I wonder if Momma knows now about David? They say no news gets across since Vicksburg fell."

"Aaron, it took seven months for this letter to catch up with us here. And you're right. Since the Yankees took Vicksburg, hardly any news or anythin' else can cross the Mississippi."

"Boys, we don't have a way to get back home, either," Pink added.

I felt the coldness come over me like I had never felt before, in spite of the September heat. We were a long way from home, but I had always supposed that I could get back home if I took a notion to do it. I felt lonely and homesick. I had seen Arkansas, Missouri,

Illinois, Ohio, Kentucky, West Virginia, Virginia and Tennessee. But the road to home was closed. I didn't talk to Noah or Pink about it. I didn't want them to think I was a baby. I was one very sad, lonely, homesick thirteen year old boy.

———————

The smell of bacon, coffee and beans lingered in the air mixed with the drifting smoke from the cooking fires. Our regiment was camped on a ridge of thick forest looking down on Chattanooga in the valley below, neatly tucked into a bend in the Tennessee River. Steamboats swarmed up and down the river. Three railroads converged there, as well as several roads. Chattanooga was a busy place. It was vital for the South to hold it.

Corporal Clint Hunter had gone with his boys down into Chattanooga to do a little shopping. They were replacing the musical instruments that had been lost at Fort Hindman. They had returned with a good used guitar, a decent fiddle, and a brand new Irish flute. Clint picked around on the guitar until he was satisfied that he had it in tune. He played the note for Josh until he painstakingly tuned each string of the fiddle. Jonathan, or Bubba, as his brothers called him, pulled out an empty wooden ammunition case and sat on top of it. They talked to each other and played a few notes back and forth. Clint nodded to Jonathan, who thumped out a rhythm on the wooden case. At the predetermined beat, the fiddle and guitar launched into a lively Irish jig. Justin picked up the tune on the flute. He played it like he had been born with it in his hand. The notes shrilled out fast and clear.

Jordy and Jamison started to dance the steps that went with the music. I had never seen Irish dancing before I met them at Personville. They had their feet flying like they were on fire, stomping out the rhythm on the hard ground, kicking out and back like they had bees in their drawers.

The music and dancing drew a crowd. Soon the whole platoon was gathered around listening, swaying and clapping. When they finished, we all clapped and hollered for more. I had been to square dances at home, but this was lots better. Jordy and Jamison were tired, so they traded out with Jonathan and Justin. They launched into an old American song called "Sally Goodin" that most of us knew. Lieutenant Kinney and Trent had joined the crowd, too. Some of the men from the rest of the company came drifting over until there was a pretty good crowd. I even noticed Captain Tyus in the back patting his foot and clapping. They kept taking turns playing and dancing until they were so tired they couldn't hit another lick. When I fell asleep that night, my homesickness was a little better.

––––––––––

Word soon came down that a large body of Union troops was heading for Chattanooga under General Rosecrans, or "Ol' Rosy." The Union forces were split into three huge columns converging on Chattanooga. The Confederate Army of Tennessee under General Braxton Bragg could easily defeat any one of the columns, but if all three united, we would be in a world of hurt. Some of the Yankee troops had already crossed the Tennessee River and were coming up behind our position. Orders came to leave Chattanooga and head south to intercept and engage this Union force while it was vulnerable.

The Texas Fifteenth Regiment had been placed in the division of the fire-eating Irishman, Patrick Cleburne. He had decided to give our regiment a chance to prove ourselves and remove the stain of Fort Hindman. I didn't see there had been a bit of shame in it. Five thousand Rebels had surrendered to thirty thousand Yankees, fifty heavy cannon and seventeen gun boats. It kind of seemed like the smart thing to do at the time. We were tired of hearing about it and were ready to prove ourselves. Colonel Deshler had full control of the regiment. We never knew what happened to Colonel Sweet.

I had ridden up and down the line carrying dispatches. It sure felt good to be on a horse again. The little dun gelding had a good set of lungs, hard black feet, and he could flat cover some ground. I had been able to figure out that the Confederate lines ran mostly north and south along Chickamauga Creek. One of the staff officers had said that was an Indian word that meant "bloody water." I could have done just fine without knowing that. The Billy Yanks were shaping up from the southwest and running mostly south to north pretty much across from our troops. General Cleburne had figured that the Yankees aimed to keep us out of Chattanooga by trying to slide to our right to cut us off, and we were supposed to push them back into the hills and all the way to the Tennessee River. General Cleburne's aide had sent me back with dispatches for Colonel Deshler and the Fifteenth. On reporting to Colonel Deshler, he gave me verbal orders to carry down the line. "Turner, Aaron Turner, isn't it, son?"

"Yes sir, Colonel Deshler." I was amazed he knew my name, but I carried reports to him often enough, I guess he had figured it out.

"Aaron, you take my orders back to every company commander from Company A to K. Aren't you in Captain Tyus' Company F, son?"

"Yes sir."

"When the bugles sound, all the companies are to advance together. They are not to allow a gap to form between any companies for any reason. You got that, son?"

"When the bugles sound, all companies are to advance together. Under no circumstances are they to allow a gap to form between companies, sir."

"Well, go then, boy. We don't pay you by the hour!"

I grinned at his little joke and put the spurs to my pretty dun horse. I galloped to each company commander until I reached Captain Tyus last of all. The horse was lathered up good and breathing hard, but I was enjoying the heck out of feeling important. The dun slid to a stop next to Captain Tyus, raising a cloud of dust I had not anticipated.

"Good night, Aaron! You're riding like a war band of Comanche are on your back trail. What's so important to raise such a sweat on your horse?"

"Sorry, Captain. I didn't mean to cause a dust storm. Colonel Deshler's compliments, sir. All companies of the Fifteenth are to advance together when the regimental bugles sound. Under no circumstances is a gap to be allowed to form between the companies, sir."

"Good job, Aaron. Now go report to Lieutenant Kinney. Unless he needs you to ride, I would suggest you loosen the cinches on your horse and let him cool a bit. It's likely to be a long day."

When I found the Lieutenant, he was on foot. Manners required that I dismount before I talked to him. It was considered disrespectful for a mounted enlisted man to speak to an officer on foot unless it was urgent. I gave him our orders.

"Alright son, you did good. It's too dangerous this close to the front for you to stay mounted, so take your horse back toward the creek. You'll find Trent there with our horses. Hobble 'em and tie 'em. We can't risk them gettin' away. Then you and Trent get back up here and bring your rifles and war bags."

———————

General Leonidas Polk, "The Fighting Bishop," commanded the north corps of Bragg's Army. Cleburne's Division anchored the southern, or left, end of Polk's Corps to the Confederate center. Our brigade was the left end of Cleburne's line, and our regiment was the left end of that line. That put us squarely across from a battle tested veteran regiment from Indiana. Rifle and cannon fire could be heard far to our left. There must be a pretty good scrap heating up to the south of us.

"Sounds like its gittin' pretty hot down there, boys. Be ready. We don't wanna let 'em have all the fun!" Sergeant Howard laughed.

Finally! Bugles sounded all along the front of Polk's Corps. Company by company, the corps began to inch forward. Our company crossed an open field on the banks of the Chickamauga heading for a stand of timber to the west. Scattered rifles shots cracked from the edge of the woods. A few men in our company fell. I didn't know if they were dead or wounded. No one in our platoon was hurt. As we approached the edge of the trees, the Yankee skirmishers fell back deeper in to the woods. The advance temporarily stalled as various regiments and companies made adjustments to stay in position.

Once again bugles sounded. The whole Corps began moving forward, pushing slowly westward. Our company was now in the woods. The Yankee skirmishers began to fire at us from behind trees close enough to do some damage. Captain Tyus ordered us into skirmish formation. This would relax the tightly packed lines we had been moving in and allow us to use what cover the country provided as we moved forward.

"Aaron, tell Sergeant Howard that I'm sendin' Sergeant Barnett's squad forward. Howard's squad is to provide cover. Trent, go tell, Sergeant Barnett." Lieutenant Kinney had a stern seriousness to his voice I had never heard before.

Second Squad, under Sergeant Barnett and Corporals Payton and Hunter scrambled to get ready. They gave a hand signal indicating they were ready.

"First Squad, pick your targets, take your time. Some of them Indiana farm boys can shoot." Obeying Sergeant Howard's orders, we raised up to where we could shoot, sheltering behind trees, stumps, and rocks. We started a steady fire into the Indiana skirmishers. Second Squad stayed low to the ground and scampered forward about twenty yards ahead of the line just to our right.

The gunpowder in the paper cartridges tasted salty as I tore the paper with my teeth and held the bullet in my mouth. I poured the powder down the barrel of my rifle and smacked the side to shake it all down to the breach. I wadded the oily paper into a ball and stuffed it into the barrel. A quick push from the metal ramrod seated the paper over the powder. Finally, I spit the bullet into the barrel and drove it home with the ramrod. I returned the ramrod to its holder and dug in my pouch for a copper percussion cap. I fumbled with it as I fit it to the nipple. I nodded to Corporal Riley that I was ready. I realized that I was the last one to get fully reloaded. He nodded to Sergeant Howard we were ready. He signaled Second Squad who opened up a covering fire while we advanced. We crawled forward until we were even with them.

It was hard to see through the yellow-gray powder smoke that hung in the still air under the trees. The smoke stunk of sulphur and burned my eyes and throat. I couldn't see the Yankees, but I knew Lieutenant Kinney and Trent were on my right, and Noah and Pink were on my left. Orange flashes stabbed through the smoke to reveal the continued presence of the Indiana men about eighty yards to the west. We dragged up tree limbs and rolled rocks to form a rough defensive line. We suspected we might be having uninvited company once the smoke cleared. We could hear shouted orders in the west.

"First Platoon, fix bayonets!" Lieutenant Kinney roared.

I fumbled around and got mine out of the scabbard and into the slot under the barrel. I never much cared for using it, as it made my rifle a little front heavy and harder to aim. I had never used it in combat. I was soon to learn its worth. Dozens of blue coated soldiers appeared like ghosts from the thinning smoke. They gave a yell and were on us.

"Wait, boys! Wait! Fire!"

Lieutenant Kinney had given the order at only twenty yards. I aimed at a big man with a black beard and squeezed the trigger. Nothing happened. I hadn't pulled the hammer to full cock. By the time I did, he was only ten yards away. The bullet took him in the belly and knocked him down. I tore another cartridge and got it started when Noah yelled.

"Aaron, look out!" A red-headed Yankee made a swipe at me with his bayonet. I rolled to my left as Lieutenant Kinney shot him dead with his revolver. I rammed the cartridge home, set the cap and remembered to cock the hammer. I saw a Yankee stop and take dead aim at the lieutenant. I shot him dead before he could pull the trigger.

Before I could reload, a Yankee ran at me with his rifle raised as a club. By instinct I sprang forward with the bayonet on the end of my rifle. The blade skittered along his breast bone before going plumb through his neck. Hot blood squirted in my face as he fell and I pulled the bayonet out. The Yankees that were left high-tailed it back to the west. I started to run after them, to strike them down, but Lieutenant Kinney grabbed my coat and held me back.

"Hold here, men. Hold here. Reload."

I saw my hands were covered with sticky blood. As I tried to ram another cartridge down the barrel I shook like a leaf in a high wind. I made sure to seat a cap, then eased the hammer back to half cocked. The line fell quiet. Corporal Riley told us to get a drink from our canteens. The tepid water loosened the powder residue in my throat, leaving an intense salty sulphur taste. I rinsed and spit until I got the worst of it out of my mouth, then drained the canteen.

Lieutenant Kinney sent Trent and me back to Chickamauga Creek to fetch water and retrieve the three horses. While we were filling the canteens, there was a terrible racket along the road as a large body of Confederate soldiers marched south along the road. Their officers turned off to water their horses across from us on Chickamauga Creek.

An officer in a major's uniform noticed us. "You boys look like you got powder on your faces. Musta been in a little scrap. Son, you hurt? You got blood all over your head and face. What unit are y'all boys with?"

"Texas Fifteenth Regiment of Cavalry, Dismounted, Company F, sir. What soldiers are those yonder, sir?"

"We brought two whole divisions down from Virginia under General Longstreet. We've come to give General Bragg a little help. That's General Longstreet yonder."

We saw a tall man with a long full beard in a magnificent uniform, mounted on a beautiful bay horse. It looked like he was conferring with his staff beside the creek.

"Well, I best be going. You Texas boys give 'em hell."

I tried to wash the blood out of my hair, off my face and hands. It made bloody streaks in the water as it flowed away from me. I remembered Chickamauga meant "bloody water." Before the day was over, it would live up to its terrible name.

9

September 19, 1863, along Chickamauga Creek

THE REST OF THE DAY WAS
pretty quiet, just a little sputtering gunfire back and
forth. We ate hard tack from our pockets and washed it
down with lukewarm water from our canteens. Captain
Tyus had said no fires tonight, which meant no coffee.
A large number of skirmishers were set out between us
and the Yankees. We didn't aim to let them sneak up on
us in the night.

I sat up and talked to Noah and Pink. I was too
wound up to go to sleep. I tried hard not to let them know
how scared I had been, or how scared I still was. It had
shaken me down to my soul to have killed men that day.
Men with faces I had seen as they died. Men who had
names I didn't know. Men who had families they would
never see again. I could still hear the sick gurgling sound
the Yankee made as my bayonet pierced his throat. I saw
the look of surprised anguish flash across the eyes of the
big man who had been aiming at Lieutenant Kinney when
I shot him dead. These images and sounds were seared
into my memory like a brand on a cow's hide. I would
carry them with me for the rest of my life.

Noah noticed the blood on me. "Aaron, you got

blood matted up in your hair and around the edges of your face. I guess I didn't notice it before. Are you hurt?"

"No. That ain't my blood."

A wave of nausea clenched my guts. I stood up just in time to turn around and puke up everything I had eaten, along with all the emotions I had been holding back all day.

"Dang it, Noah. No, I'm not alright. A thousand damn Yankees tried to kill me today. I killed three of them. I shot one in the belly that was aimmin' at me. I shot one that was tryin' to shoot the lieutenant. I ran my bayonet in the throat of a Yankee who was tryin' to club me with his rifle. I reckon I'm not alright. I feel worse than I ever felt in my life. I'm still shakin'. I don't know which is worse, somebody tryin' to kill me, or killin' somebody else."

Noah and Pink looked away. Scalding hot tears rolled down my bloody face. Nobody talked for a while. Pink finally spoke up.

"Aaron, I didn't say anythin' to you earlier. I wanted you to think I was steady as a rock through the whole deal. I feel just like you do. My hands are still shakin'. I can't get the faces of the men I killed out of my mind. While you were gone to fetch water, me and Noah was both pukin' our guts up. Most of the platoon was, too. I don't think any of us killed anybody before, at least not where we could see their faces. This was up close and personal. You and Noah both did real good today."

I thought back to that day when we enlisted. We all had new uniforms, and there were flags flying. It seemed like we were leaving for the greatest adventure of our lives.

Now I had another man's blood matted in my hair. Nobody could have told me what it would feel like to kill a man. I wouldn't have understood the cold chill when somebody is trying to kill me, or the excitement when I killed them first. I couldn't explain it to anyone. But I realized that Noah and Pink knew what I felt. The other men in our platoon probably felt the same way. But it wasn't something that I could put into words.

I had been tested that day in the fires of war. I hadn't run away. I stood my ground and fought. This had changed me. I felt as if something of mine had been violently taken away. Maybe it was the innocence of youth that was gone. I felt like a normal thirteen year old boy this morning. I would never be that same boy again. I sensed that I had been forcefully reshaped into something different. I couldn't describe it. I hadn't changed from good to evil, or gone from young to old. My heart had been heated in the fire of battle and hammered by violence into something different. I felt hardness in my heart. There was a deep sadness in my soul. The boy who had ridden out of Texas was gone and a man I didn't quite know had taken his place.

The breaking rays of the morning sun showed that the Yankees had withdrawn to the Lafayette Road a few miles west of their position the night before. It was the main overland route from Chattanooga to Lafayette, Georgia. The roadbed had eroded deeply into the red earth over the years, making it a natural defensive position.

"Hey, Pink, you reckon the Yankees run off?"

"Naw. They ain't near whipped. I guess they just moved back to a better spot for fightin'."

You think we'll git into Georgia anytime soon?"

"We been in Georgia, on and off, the last two days!"

"I thought we were still in Tennessee. When did we get to Georgia?"

Before he could explain that the battlefield wrapped across the state line, Sergeant Howard came by to tell us we could light cooking fires. He told us to eat good, because we were going to be ordered forward later in the day. Ham and Ky Howard came around pretty soon with some bacon, hard tack and real coffee. Ky said they had "borrowed it from the Yankee commissary."

I guess that was about the best coffee I had in a long time. We fried up extra bacon and put it in our coat pockets, along with all the hard tack we could carry. We needed to top off our canteens. The sergeant had taught us to "water up good" every chance we got. We didn't know when we might get to eat or drink again.

Lieutenant Kinney sent Trent and me back to refill everyone's canteens. We got to ride this time, which sure beat walking. About an hour after we got back, we could hear rifle fire at the far north end of General Polk's Corps. Captain Tyus sent me to ride up to Colonel Deshler for news.

I found him without too much trouble about a mile north of our company. "Captain Tyus' compliments, sir."

"Yes, Private?"

"Captain Tyus reports that Company F is ready to advance and awaiting orders, sir."

"Private, you're the third courier with the same report. Everybody is impatient, includin' me. Don't bother ridin' up to division headquarters, son. General Cleburne doesn't know either. General Polk can't seem to make up his mind when we're to advance. Have you been hearin' that fightin' goin' on to the north end of the line?"

"Yes, sir. We've been wonderin' about that."

"There's a pretty hot little skirmish goin' on up there between a big Yankee cavalry patrol, fightin' dismounted, against some of our boys. The Yankees have got Spencer rifles and are givin' our boys all they can handle."

"Beggin' the Colonel's pardon, sir. What's a Spencer rifle?"

"Here, I'll show you this one. Someone got it from a Yankee trooper yesterday and gave it to me." He pulled a strange looking rifle out of a leather scabbard. "It shoots a .56 caliber bullet from a copper rimfire cartridge. You pull this lever down, it opens the breech and slides in a cartridge. Pull it back and it closes the breech. Cock the hammer, pull the trigger. It shoots seven times before you reload. It has this tube magazine which fits in the butt stock of the gun. When it's empty, just slide it out, push in another tube, and you're ready to go. You can load it on Sunday and shoot all week."

"I gotta get me one of those, Colonel!"

"When you steal one off a Yankee, you better steal plenty of cartridges, because that's the only way to get them. Now, you ride back to Captain Tyus and tell him Billy Yank is dug in along the

Lafayette Road with log breastworks. When the bugles finally sound, your company is to advance and attack the position along the road, but to maintain contact with the units on either side. We don't want to give those Blue bellies a hole to attack through. You got that, Tex?"

I returned his grin with a smart salute. "Yes sir, Colonel Deshler, sir!"

"Take this Spencer and this tin of magazines. It's full of thirteen tubes of seven shots each. I don't intend to get close enough to need it."

"Thank you very much, sir!" I attached the scabbard and magazine box to my horse, being careful to hang on to my Enfield rifle. I spurred my horse back to Captain Tyus riding like a drunk Comanche.

―――――――――

The bugles sounded about ten o'clock. Polk's Corps advanced at a walk through the fields and forests. When the huge line came grinding to a halt, the Fifteenth Texas Regiment was about seventy yards from the Lafayette Road in the edge of some timber. In our front, the Yankees had piled logs on the eastern edge of the road facing us. Behind them, across the road, and up a little slope, they had placed a few light field guns. They had made some half-built sand bag protection around the cannon and their crews.

We opened a general fire on their line to get an idea of how many men were there. Sergeant Howard said there was more than enough to go around. We could see the flag of the Indiana regiment we had fought yesterday, plus another each from Iowa and Illinois. I didn't know what the rest of the line looked like, but this was more than we could handle.

I got sent galloping back to Colonel Deshler. He read the dispatch and sent me urgently on to Divisional Headquarters to find General Cleburne. I addressed a major near the general. "Fifteenth Texas Regiment, Colonel Deshler's compliments, sir."

The red faced major was none too friendly. "What is it, boy?"

"Colonel Deshler reports that our regiment is facin' regiments from Iowa, Indiana, and Illinois. He requests reinforcements if the General expects the Fifteenth to advance, sir."

General Patrick Cleburne, "The Fighting Irishman," wheeled his horse and walked it next to mine. "Red hair, blue eyes. Are ye Irish, lad?"

"My people, on both my mother's and my father's families, came from Ireland better than a hundred years ago, sir."

"I knew I could spot a good Irish lad. Do you like the life of a soldier, son?"

"I believe in servin' Texas, sir. And my platoon has become like family. But, no, I don't like the killin' part, sir."

"Well spoken, lad. If you ever got to likin' the killin' part you wouldn't be a child of God, but of the Devil himself. You tell my friend, Colonel Deshler, I'll be sendin' General Govan's whole Arkansas Brigade to reinforce him. Once they are there, General Govan will be in command. They are to attack once the reinforcements are in place. Tell me your name, lad."

"Private Aaron Turner, Fifteenth Texas, sir."

"Mary, Joseph and Patrick guard you, Aaron Turner."

———————

Govan's Arkansas Brigade was composed of three over strength regiments. Once they were in position, the Brigade's buglers sounded the charge. Our combined force of roughly five thousand men charged the entrenched three thousand Yankees defending the road.

Cannon barked from across the road, their loads of grape shot tearing holes in our lines. General Govan had detailed his best marksmen to silence the gun crews. They fell like turkeys shot from the roost. With the Rebel yell rising in a great crescendo from five thousands throats, we rushed against the breastworks and fought bayonet to bayonet over the logs.

Skeet and Ham Howard were the strongest men I had ever

known. They grabbed the ends of a huge cottonwood log from the breastworks and plowed into the mass of blue uniforms filling the road. The log flattened everyone in its path. Their family came behind, bayoneting the fallen Yankees. This created a breach in the Union lines, and dozens of Rebel soldiers poured into the opening. The Yankees fought back fiercely for a brief while, but as more Confederates poured into the breach, they finally broke and retreated into the woods beyond the road. They fled to the right, the left and center. This opened a gap through which the rest of the brigade poured to exploit the opportunity. Those Billy Yanks who fled down the road to the right or the left were cut down by the massed men firing into their ranks above the road. Those who fled up the gentle hill were brought down with the cold steel of bayonets in their backs.

The Union line that had appeared so formidable evaporated before us. General Govan had us shift the logs to the opposite side of the road. We turned the Yankee six pounder cannon around to defend our position and built protection for the guns and their crews.

I was sent to General Cleburne with the report. The Union left flank had collapsed at its center. Confederate forces were firmly in place. He sent more troops to exploit the breach. We repelled several determined Union counter attacks, but maintained our position on the Lafayette Road. The reinforcements expanded the breach both right and left.

The collapse of this portion of the Federal line caused Union Commander, General Rosecrans, to send an entire Union Corps against our four regiments to reclaim the road. The road was their vital link to their true objective of Chattanooga. This shift of troops away from the center of the main Union line would have disastrous results for the Yankees.

As the fresh troops pressed on us, I had the opportunity to use my Spencer rifle. It lacked the kick of the Enfield, but it could fire a bullet every three seconds. It was easy to insert a fresh tube of cartridges. But before I could fire more than fourteen shots, it was time to head to the woods. The Yankees could have pursued us if they had a mind to do it, but they were as tired as we were. They had regained possession of the road. Captain Tyus had the sergeants to muster each platoon. We had lost Joseph Evans, Brendan Moss and Tobe Howard. Thank God, Noah and Pink were uninjured. We huddled in the edge of the woods hoping the Yankees would not attack.

———————

The Yankees knew where we were and there were enough skirmishers out to keep us from being surprised, so the order came down that cooking fires were to be allowed. Lieutenant Kinney sent us out to do a little scavenging from the battlefield behind us to see if we could scratch up some things we could use. Noah and Pink went with me to keep me company. We each carried a couple of empty tow sacks for food, cartridges, or anything handy. Most of what we found had been trampled into the ground. We did find two unopened tins of coffee, some tins of peaches, a sack of hard tack, a small sack of sugar and a side of bacon in a canvas bag.

I spotted something near a dead Confederate officer. "Pink, come look at this." It was a nine shot .44 caliber revolver. Instead of a cylinder pin, it rotated around a twenty gauge shotgun barrel. There was a simple lever on the hammer that could be flipped to fire either the cylinder or the shotgun barrel. It was long and heavy.

"Aaron, I've seen one of these before. It's a LeMatt revolver, made in New Orleans. They're expensive, about $200. That shotgun barrel is usually loaded with buckshot. See if he has got any extra cartridges and caps on him."

We rolled the gray-clad corpse over to find a gaping hole where a face should be. We covered his head up so we wouldn't have to look at the grotesque sight. We found a holster for the LeMatt, a pocketful of paper cartridges, percussion caps, and a tobacco pouch full of buckshot. He had a good pair of boots that would fit Noah. We took them, as the gentleman would not need them anymore. I found two Spencer rifles and a full canister of magazine tubes for each. Noah found two Colt Navy .44 revolvers. He also found a nearly full container of paper cartridges for the pistols.

We were pretty proud of our haul of goods until we heard a groan come from one of the Yankees lying on his back on the ground. He looked about eighteen. His cap showed he was from the Indiana unit we had been fighting.

I knelt down next to him. "Billy Yank, you alive?"

He opened his eyes and looked around at us. "Water."

There was a dead soldier near him with a full canteen which we grabbed. Pink gently raised the injured soldier up to where he could drink. He took several long swallows. "Thanks. Name is Tom Williams from Indiana. You boys Rebs?"

"Yeah. We'll send for somebody to take care of you."

"Don't waste your time; I'm done. I wrote a letter to my mother. It's in my coat pocket. Will you get it to someone in the Indiana regiment? They'll send it home to her."

"Sure, Tom, I'll do it." I fished the addressed envelope out of his pocket and put it in mine.

He reached out his hand to shake mine. "Thanks, Johnny Reb." His eyes closed and he drifted away.

"Aaron, what are you gonna do with that letter?" Noah asked.

"I don't know. I'll figure out somethin'."

We realized that Pink wasn't with us. We could see him a way off, cutting the haunches from a freshly killed mule. He looked up as he wiped the blood off his bayonet. "We're gonna have some good groceries tonight!"

———————

We returned to camp with bounty collected from the field. Pink and Noah would each keep a Navy Colt, and I would keep the LeMatt. We shared out the food and cartridges. I took a can of peaches to Captain Tyus. He gave us permission to build a fire to roast our late night snack. We shared the other cans among our platoon. Nobody got much, but everyone got some. We roasted the mule hindquarters over a hot bed of oak coals. We rubbed them down with salt while they cooked. We made several large pots of coffee to share while the meat cooked. Anyone who wanted it could have a little sugar in his coffee.

The smell of the roasting meat drew everybody from the platoon around the fire. Corporal Hunter sent Josh and Jonathan back to the supply wagons across Chickamauga Creek to fetch their instruments. It wasn't long until they were tuned up and playing their hearts out.

We sat around the cooking fire, sipping good coffee with a pinch of sugar, listening to the music. The Hunters were too tired to dance a lick, but they played like angels. The meat smelled so tempting, we talked Pink into slicing off pieces that were cooked enough to eat from the outside. He put his bayonet to good use filling plates as we passed them to him. We each grabbed a piece and shared it out with the others. The mule meat was coarser than beef, but sweeter and very good. We ate all that we could hold and shared out what was left with the other platoons in the company. We took a couple of especially good portions to Lieutenant Kinney and Captain Tyus. I rolled out my blankets next to Pink and Noah and thought of all the things that had happened since we had left Texas. I felt better than I had earlier. I fell asleep dreaming of Momma and our home on the Navasota River. I hadn't slept long before I woke up and remembered there was something I had to do.

———

Once the fighting died down that night, the brigade had sent out a heavy group of skirmishers. I quietly left camp and slipped out among the skirmishers.

"Where y'all from?"

"Arkansas. What about you?"

"Texas Fifteenth. We fought with y'all on the Lafayette Road today."

"Sure did. Them boys in yore bunch that picked up that log busted a hole in the Yankee lines big as a barn. We ran their blue bellies off, until so many of 'em came back with reinforcements. Then we had to high tail it out of there. What are you doin' way off over here, Texas boy?"

"I was scavengin' the battlefield from where we fought earlier today. I found me a Yankee soldier that weren't quite dead. We give him some water, but it was easy to see he was goin' down fast. He had a letter wrote to his Ma in Indiana. I promised I'd git it to some Yanks to mail to her. I'm pretty sure that those are Indiana boys across the way."

"Yeah, it is. We talk a little to 'em. Yore gonna fool around and git yourself shot, is what yore gonna do."

"I don't aim to; I been shot at enough already today."

"Well, give 'em a holler and see what happens."

"Billy Yank! Hey, Billy Yank! I want to talk."

"I hear ya Johnny Reb. I ain't takin' none of your tricks!"

"No tricks, Yank. I'm Private Aaron Turner, Fifteenth Texas. A wounded Yankee give me a letter for his Ma before he died. I promised I'd git it to you Indiana boys."

"What you want me to do about it?"

"I reckon git it to an officer to mail it home. It's got an address on it."

A different voice responded. "Private Turner, you come out here where we can see ya. Hold up a white shirt or something. No gun. I'll pass the order for my men not to shoot. I'm Captain Jacob Richburg, Fourth Indiana. Make sure your men don't shoot at us."

I looked for the commanding officer of the Confederate skirmishers, but didn't see him. "Hey, Arkie, where's your officer?"

"I'm right behind you, son. I heard the whole thing. Captain Richburg? This is Captain Hiram Combs, First Arkansas Infantry, Govan's Brigade. I'll order my men to hold their fire."

"Agreed. Fourth Indiana, hold your fire." The order was repeated down the line.

"Captain Combs, what this boy is doing is above the call of duty. In appreciation, I'm sending over a sack of coffee beans."

"Thank you, Captain Richburg. First Arkansas, hold your fire. Captain Richburg, I'm sendin' a good sized sack of prime cured tobacco for you boys to enjoy before we try to kill ya tomorrow."

He handed me a tow sack of fragrant tobacco. "Git going, Private, this was your idea."

I walked slowly, holding a white rag and the tobacco. I watched as a young man in a blue uniform stepped out of the shadows and walked toward me. He was holding a white rag on a stick, and had a big sack over his shoulder. We met in the middle. I set down the tobacco and he set down the coffee beans.

"Howdy, Yank. Name's Aaron Turner, from Texas. I offered my hand which he accepted with a firm shake.

"You Rebs sure been makin' it hot for us today. Name is Jimmy Tullis from Indiana. I brung you a ten pound bag of coffee beans. Captain Richburg said to sure thank you for bringin' that letter."

"I got this sack of tobacco for you. It smells like prime stuff. Here's the letter. I didn't know what to do with it."

"We'll make sure it gets to his mother. You Rebs gettin' tired yet?"

"No, were just gettin' goin' good. There's so dang many of us, we have to take turns fightin'."

"You Texans can lie with the best of 'em. I better git goin'." We shook hands again and grabbed our new sacks and trotted back to our own lines.

"Thank you, Captain Combs. The truce is over now."

"Captain Richburg, thanks for the coffee. We was plannin' on stealin' some in the mornin' but you saved us the trouble. I reckon we can go back to killin' each other now."

"Aaron, you got more guts than brains. You take that coffee with you and git back on up to your company before they think you deserted."

———

Morning came with no new orders. The sun was high by the time "The Fighting Bishop" decided to fight. He finally sent orders for the Corps to advance and engage the enemy all along the front.

The Fifteenth Texas was fighting over the same ground we had fought for the day before. We opened up with our rifles from the cover of the woods east of the Lafayette Road. We kept up a pretty hot fire at the Union position. I liked the way the Spencer handled. I took my time, aiming my shots. I could shoot fourteen times for every two shots the boys with the Enfield rifles took, but I slowed that down so I wouldn't burn up all my cartridges. I was next to Noah and Pink. They were cranking it out with their Spencers, too. Lieutenant Kinney and Trent were just off my right elbow. The attack slowed to a good simmering fire from both sides. Neither one seemed inclined to push it any harder.

About noon, a rider came from the south. General Longstreet's Corps had found a gap in the Union lines. The brigade that had been pulled out of line yesterday to reinforce the Yankees we were fighting had left a big hole in the Federal position. Longstreet's skirmishers had found it before the Union had time to close the gap. The whole Virginia Corps had poured through the breach and had savaged the Union right flank. The Union center and right collapsed and were being rolled up like a carpet. They were in full retreat for Chattanooga.

Union Major General George Thomas, without waiting for orders from General Rosecrans, organized a fighting retreat to the heights of Horseshoe Ridge. He gathered what remained of the Union center and all of the left flank fighting along the Lafayette Road. He had them fall back to the ridge. Longstreet's Corps pursued the fleeing Yankee army. The men in gray were exhausted from the morning's fight and were not able to stop the Federal troops before they reached Chattanooga. General Polk threw his Corps against the Yankees who had turned to fight on Horseshoe Ridge.

We threw ourselves in attack after attack up the steep wooded slope, but weren't able to dislodge our enemies in blue. By dusk, we were firmly anchored all along the foot of Horseshoe Ridge, but the Stars and Stripes still flew over the battered Union position.

During the night, General Thomas, who would forever be known as "The Rock of Chickamauga," silently withdrew his troops over the rocky crest of the hill and away to the safety of Chattanooga.

He had stopped the wholesale slaughter of the Rosecrans' Army of the Cumberland.

We had met the enemy and driven them in disarray from the field of battle at a terrible cost in Union and Confederate lives. It was a decisive Southern victory, but the Union held Chattanooga and the South did not. It was a hollow victory. Much blood had been spilled and many lives thrown away to win a battle, and yet lost the city and its railroads that held the key to the survival of the Confederacy.

I had shown myself, at thirteen years of age, unafraid in battle, but sickened with killing. I lost something of myself along the bloody waters of Chickamauga Creek, but found something within myself I did not yet understand.

10

Late September, 1863, Billy Goat Hill, above Chattanooga, Tennessee

        WE HAD TAKEN OUR TIME getting back to Chattanooga. By the time we got there, "Ol' Rosy" and the Yankees had set up shop mighty well. They could get supplies by railroad and steamboat. General Bragg had us spread out in the hills above Chattanooga, which was nestled in a bend of the Tennessee River curving through the valley below us. The south end of the Confederate line was anchored at Lookout Mountain. Cannon had been mounted there that pretty well shut down both the railroad and the river traffic. Most of General Bragg's forces were strung out along Missionary Ridge. It ran mostly south to north. The side facing Chattanooga was very steep and forested. Rifle pits had been dug at the foot of the slope and ever so often up the sides to the top. Cannon had been placed here which commanded the valley below. Our division under General Patrick Cleburne anchored the north end of the line across a gap from Missionary Ridge on a mountain called Billy Goat Hill. We had trenches dug and reinforced with logs. Cannon were placed to sweep the approaches to our position.

We only had a handful of tents. Most of us made dugouts in the slope behind the earthworks. Branches held up a canvas roof and sides. Shallow trenches directed the runoff away from the tent. The frequent rains blew in under the canvas and kept our things damp. Even on the hilltop, the mosquitoes could get bad on still nights. I was convinced it rained more in Tennessee than anywhere in the world. We had to work cleaning our guns daily and tried to keep the cartridges dry. We were supplied pretty generously from the Federal commissary. The Yankees kept sending wagon trains of supplies down some of the small roads into Chattanooga, and our cavalry did a real good job of stopping most of them. We ate Yankee hard tack, salt pork, beans and cornmeal washed down with Yankee coffee most of the time.

The Army of Tennessee had a right smart of men at Chattanooga, but we just sat up in the hills and watched it rain and ate free food from the Union grocery store. I had wondered why we didn't attack, but a thirteen year old private doesn't cut much ice with the generals. We settled into a routine of manning the trenches all day with a few people on duty at night. Different companies got to take turns skirmishing down the side of the mountain. I liked it when it was our turn for skirmish duty. It got me out of the muddy trenches where I could sit on a rock or a stump and watch for Yankees, rabbits and deer. There wasn't many of any of those to be found.

On one of the days of skirmish duty, the day was clear and dry. The trees had just a hint of the color to come later. Noah and I sat under a big hickory tree and talked about home.

"Hey, Noah. You reckon they're pickin' cotton at home yet?"

"Nope. It's too early yet. There won't likely be a killin' frost there for another six weeks yet. I bet they've got the corn in and are diggin' taters."

"Wouldn't some baked sweet potatoes with a dab of fresh butter and salt taste good? Or a skillet of fried potatoes and onions?"

"With a big ol' plate of biscuits, with butter and sorghum molasses, and a big glass of cool buttermilk. This army grub ain't much to brag about, is it."

"You reckon Momma and Mary Ann are makin' it ok?"

"I guess so. Chavez and Lucio can manage the farm pretty well. They'll watch after Momma, too. Of course, the sheriff and Mr. Morgan live close by. They promised to check on them pretty often. Then Marcus and Lucius are just over at Personville if somebody needs 'em. I think they'll be alright."

"This soldierin' ain't turned out to be much fun, has it little brother. I hadn't seen a parade since we left Texas or a brass band playin'. It's pretty much just hurry up and wait."

Yeah, I know. I hasn't been what I expected either, especially that prison camp. I sure miss Davey."

"Me, too. Tell ya the truth, Aaron, I miss Momma and home pretty bad right now. Every time I get to thinkin' on a way to get back home, I can't come up with a single way to do it with the war going. We can't get home 'til it's over. I don't see that happenin' any time soon. I'm not so sure about us winnin' this war, either. I think the South has bit off more than it can chew."

"We won at Chickamauga, didn't we?"

"Yeah, and the Yankees are holdin' Chattanooga."

We fell silent in a grumpy, gloomy mood. A red squirrel came rustling through the leaves on the ground looking for hickory nuts. He stopped and raised up to stare at us just a second too long. Noah chunked a rock at him and by pure chance, hit that sucker in the head. He had knocked him out cold. We ran over there to put him one of our forage sacks.

"Aaron, I got an idea. Let's sack up 'Mister Squirrel' and take him back to camp. I intend to have a little fun with Taylor Edwards tonight."

Back at camp after supper, the Hunters played awhile for us before people started heading off to bed. We had put the squirrel in Taylor's bedroll with the top of the tow sack folded down. Directly, Taylor crawled in bed and moved the sack just enough that the squirrel got loose. It didn't appreciate the way it had been treated and was looking for a way to get even and get out. That squirrel ran up his leg, across his chest and bit him on the end of the nose. The screaming and cussing was loud enough to wake up the whole camp. It was a race to see if Taylor or the squirrel was going to get out of that tent first. Taylor ran hollering out the tent flap in his long drawers, but the squirrel bolted and passed him. We decided the squirrel had won "by a nose." We laughed until our sides hurt.

The Yankees were successful in reopening one of the rail lines into Chattanooga. Soon, we found ourselves facing an additional twenty thousand Federal soldiers. I heard Colonel Deshler say that the Union had sent a man called Grant to be the head general and brought in his second-in-command, a General Sherman. The Colonel said he didn't know much about either one of them. He didn't seem too concerned. He should have been worried. The days were coming when those names would arouse anger and genuine fear in all of us.

On November 23, 1863, the Yankees pushed eastward out of Chattanooga and over ran the Confederate skirmishers on two little hills in the valley, Brushy Knob and Orchard Knob. The boys in gray simply fell back to the rifle pits at the base of Missionary Ridge.

The next day, the Yankees led a heavy attack against Lookout Mountain. The artillery on top of the mountain had been situated to cover the river, the railroad and the valley floor. The cannon gave the Yankees a bad time of it until they got close to the base of the mountain. The guns could not be repositioned to direct fire at them. The blue coated soldiers swarmed up the lower parts of the hill. After a hot, day-long battle, the South still held the top of the mountain, but their big guns were useless. The Union troops were in a position to sweep them away by morning. The Confederates abandoned their stronghold during the night. They managed to take most of their guns with them. Retreating across Chattanooga Creek, they took up new positions at the foot of Missionary Ridge, burning the bridges behind them.

The following day, General Sherman led a heavy attack against those of us in Cleburne's Division on Billy Goat Hill. We had cut the timber and brush down and hauled it away to give us a clear firing line for two hundred yards in front of our trenches. With the trees and underbrush gone, there would be no cover for the attacking Yankees. Our skirmishers in the woods slowed up Sherman's troops long enough for us to get ready. I was running messages on foot all the way to division headquarters.

General Cleburne stopped to talk to me. "Well, it's my Irish soldier from Texas. What's your name again, lad?"

"Aaron Turner, sir, Fifteenth Texas, Company F."

"I see you still have that fancy Spencer rifle and a revolver, too. Are you plannin' on killin' some Yankees?"

"Only if I have to, sir."

"Take this message to Colonel Deshler: You must hold your position at all costs. Did you get that, Aaron?"

"Yes, sir. Hold position at all costs."

"Mary, Joseph and Patrick go with you, son."

———————

I ran back to Colonel Deshler at regimental command. He sent me on with orders to Captain Tyus. He sent me on down the chain of command to Lieutenant Kinney. "Captain Tyus compliments, sir. The company is to hold the line at all costs."

"Get Noah and Pink over here. Go get Sergeants Howard and Barnett, then you fall in line here between your brothers and me."

The sergeants reported, bringing the corporals with them. "Sergeants, get your men ready. We're in for it. The whole regiment has been ordered to hold at all costs. We need every man that can hold a rifle on the line, every cook, teamster, and sick or wounded that can stand up. Wait for my orders to open fire." We could see blue uniforms in the edge of the woods two hundred yards away.

Colonel Deshler sent word that the regiment's artillery was

to engage the enemy with grape shot. When they were within one hundred yards, they were to switch to canister. The cannon, which were scattered up and down the line of the regiment, burst into life, belching out uncounted thousands of one pound iron shot. The big guns tore into the packed Yankees like massive hammer strokes. The thick, yellow gray sulphur smoke clouded the battlefield and burned my eyes and throat.

Bugles answered from the forest. Thousands of Yankees surged forward. The cannon continued to chew gaping holes in their approaching line, only to be replaced with more Yankees from the rear. When they reached a hundred yards, the deadly work of the canister shot began. Each tin cylinder erupted from the cannon barrel to rip open, spewing hundreds of musket balls like the world's largest shotgun. Men fell like they had been mowed down by an enormous scythe. The blue line wavered, then continued unevenly. Captain Tyus had us hold our fire until the Yankees were within twenty yards. A bugle sang out, and we began to pour aimed rifle shot into the blue lines from a range from where we couldn't miss. Noah, Pink and I, as well as several of the other men, hurriedly worked the levers on our Spencer rifles. The combination of canister shot and well aimed rifle fire broke the Yankee advance. When recall was sounded, their decimated ranks broke and ran for the woods. The cannon switched back to grape shot, driving the Union soldiers deeper into the trees. The shot splintered trees all around them. The very forest that had provided shelter was beginning to topple around them. A cheer echoed up and down our line, but we knew that the Yankees were far from beaten.

The Union troops regrouped and charged again and again. One especially strong surge reached the edge of the trenches. Bayonets and pistols had driven them back. A mountain of a man in a blue uniform leapt over the log on top of our trench and struck at Noah with his bayonet. I put a bullet from my LeMatt into his back from point blank range. Another Yankee had forced his way into the trench and shoved me all the way across the muddy ditch. He lunged with his bayonet. I flipped the hammer lever on the LeMatt to fire the shotgun barrel.

The load of buckshot from only inches away exploded his face into a red mist as his dead body collapsed on top of me.

Several Yankees breached the line in front of Sergeant Barnett's squad. His son, Ethan, was strong as an ox and fought like a bear. He and his father fought side by side. Dead Yankees piled up around them. The Barnett's bayonets ran red with blood. As they were engaged in desperate fighting, a Union officer reached the top of the trench and shot them both dead with a revolver. Corporal Hunter and his son, Josh, enraged by the death of their friends, killed the officer with their bayonets. Jonathan, Jordan, Justin and Jamison pushed into the weakened area. The addition of their strength and fury at the critical moment drove the Yankees back from the Confederate line. When it looked like we could take no more, four companies of Govan's Arkansas Brigade that had been held in reserve charged into the fight. The added strength turned the tide and the Yankees were driven from the field to return no more.

While we had repelled the Yankees on Billy Goat Hill, the battle raged along Missionary Ridge. Union General Thomas, the "Rock of Chickamauga," had been given the task of taking the rifle pits at the base of the steep ridge. His men, remembering their previous rough treatment by the Confederates, charged through the cannon shot falling like hailstones from the top of the ridge. They stormed the rifle pits with fury and vengeance. They completely swarmed over the Rebel defenders, sending the survivors scrambling up the hill to the next line of trenches. Without orders, the Yankees continued up the slope so quickly they overran trench after trench sending the Confederate troops retreating for the safety of the mountain top. General Bragg had thought the steep terrain and trenches would play a huge factor in defense of the ridge. He was so convinced of the security of the position there that he had removed some of the defending forces for an attempted flanking movement that never occurred. Thomas' men swept over every line of defense, sustaining terrible causalities. Seeing the unexpected success of the unplanned attack, Grant rushed reinforcements to Missionary Ridge. The Confederate cannon were situated to fire at the valley below, and couldn't be redirected to fire down the slope. Trench by trench, the Yankees pushed up the steep slope. In places, the ground was slick with the blood of men clad both in blue and gray. The impregnable anchor of the entire Confederate position was swept away. By late afternoon, the Stars and Stripes flew atop the ridge. The main body of the Confederate army was in full retreat. Orders arrived that Cleburne's Division was to cover the retreat and form a rear guard.

Our division had won a hard fought victory, but the rest of the Confederate Army had crumbled. Chattanooga, its railroads, river ports and highways, was in Union hands. Our defeated army was all that stood between the invading Federal army and the approaches to Atlanta.

11

Late November, 1863, mountains of northwestern Georgia

THE RETREATING SOUTHERN army poured through the mountains of Georgia over Taylor's Ridge at a place called Ringgold Gap. Colonel Deshler had been transferred. Our new commander was a Colonel Smith. We were still part of General Cleburne's Division. Because of the fighting at Chickamauga, and especially at Billy Goat Hill, our division had earned the distinction of being recognized as crack troops. We had come a long way from the cat calls of only a few weeks ago. The stain of Fort Hindman, as undeserved as it was, was washed away in blood.

"You boys know that some of the rest of the Army of Tennessee are callin' Cleburne's Division the toughest unit in Bragg's army?" Pink asked.

"I heard. I can't believe those Yankees stormed right up Missionary Ridge and cost us the whole shootin' match!" Noah complained.

I sat thinking for a while. "All I know is that while Bragg and the rest of the Confederate Army are skedaddlin' for Dalton, we got left behind to slow down the whole stinkin' Union army."

After Sergeant Barnett had been killed at Chattanooga, Corporal Harold Payton had been made Sergeant of Second Squad, and Calvin Anderson had taken his place as Corporal. Colonel Smith had us digging trenches at the top of Ringgold Gap and rolling artillery into place. The Yankees could take this place if they wanted it bad enough, but it was going to cost them.

––––––––

The late fall and early winter of 1863 were hard on us. We had inadequate tents and blankets for the cold wet weather in the mountains of northwestern Georgia. We had to move often to keep our army between the Yankees and Atlanta. We didn't have time to build much in the way of shelter. We would mound up dirt on a patch of higher ground if we could find it. Branches held up the mildewed and rotting canvas. We were cold and damp most of the time.

My brogans had grown too small and were worn out. In spite of our less than generous rations, I had grown to over six feet tall and around one hundred and forty pounds. Noah had finally stopped growing at six foot three inches and maybe one hundred and seventy pounds. He still had the boots he had scavenged from the battlefield at Chickamauga, but the soles were gone. He got a piece of green cowhide from the butcher and cut two pieces to wrap around his boots with the hair side in. When the rawhide shrunk to the boots, it made serviceable repairs. They were kind of odd looking, and Noah had such big feet the men took to referring to them as "Noah's Arks."

As we were settling in to defend Ringgold Gap, a cavalry patrol captured a big Union supply wagon train with lots of food, blankets, canvas, clothes and boots. I got a pair of boots that fit just right, a new pair of blue wool pants, some warm woolen drawers, and a blue coat. Noah and Pink got the things they needed, plus a large piece of fresh canvas. We appreciated the Yankees generosity. I wondered how long we could get by stealing our supplies.

––––––––

The Yankees sent major General "Fightin' Joe" Hooker and three whole divisions against our one at Ringgold Gap. The shape of the mountains and the pass prevented any flanking maneuvers, and it would take three days of hard marching to go around us. They decided just to try to waltz over us in direct frontal attacks up the long slope.

The Yankees came in waves, and we killed them in waves. Our Spencer rifles came in mighty handy. Several of the other men in the company had picked up Spencers after the Union retreat at Billy Goat Hill. We had cleaned out the Yankees' pockets of cartridges and reloading tubes. Noah, Pink and I had all the Spencer cartridges we could carry, plus extra for our Enfield rifles and .44 caliber revolvers. I had relieved a dead Federal of a war bag full of fresh hard tack, dried fruit, sugar, a tin of coffee, and $23 in silver coins. I didn't know why he had carried it into battle, but we were sure glad he did.

The Union attacks never quite reached our trenches. Their artillery didn't do much damage from their position at the foot of the pass, but what big guns we had did their job well. Along about dusk General Cleburne sent orders that we were to make a good show of building fires and cooking supper. The quartermasters made sure we all had plenty of bacon and coffee. The breeze carried the tempting scent down the slope to the battered Union forces. After full dark, General Cleburne began pulling one company after another out of line and down the back slope of Ringgold Gap. By midnight, only our brightly burning fires were left along the trenches. The entire division slipped away and rejoined the Army of Tennessee. We had successfully held up the Federal advance long enough for the Confederate forces to reorganize, regroup and escape. The battle of Ringgold Gap would go down in the books as a victory for Cleburne's fabled division.

————————

The Army of Tennessee had fallen back past Dalton, Georgia, to a little railroad and sawmill town known as Resaca. The Yankees were coming through the mountain valleys in three separate corps of over thirty thousand men each. General Bragg, having displeased President Jefferson Davis, was transferred to guard duty at a post office or something. He had not been very popular with the soldiers and we were not sad to see him go. General Joseph Johnston was sent to replace him.

General Johnston had a reputation for taking care of his soldiers and not throwing away their lives carelessly. He had been given command of forty-five thousand men at Resaca, along with a large amount of artillery and an additional ten thousand crack cavalry under General Joseph Wheeler.

I overheard General Cleburne telling his staff that Johnston's Army could defeat any one of the Federal corps. But, if they ever combined forces, we would have our hands full. Johnston assigned Cleburne's Division to General Hardee's Corps. This corps was placed on a high ridge running east to west just south of Camp Creek. The small sleepy town of Resaca lay behind the ridge we defended. The Conasauga River protected our right, or east, flank, as did the Oostanaula River on the west. The ridge was lined with artillery which could sweep the whole battlefield before us, and could still be adjusted to fire down the slope in front of us. Somebody had learned something at Missionary Ridge. General Leonidas Polk, who had commanded our corps at Chickamauga, had gathered reinforcements in Mississippi and arrived with a whole division of fresh troops. His division was positioned to shield the west flank of the ridge. General Wheeler's cavalry secured the east flank.

"Noah, where in the world did these Georgia crackers come up with the names for some of these rivers and creeks? Some of 'em sound like a disease or somethin'."

"I guess they're some sort of Indian names."

"Well, at least the places around home have American or Mexican names we can pronounce."

"You mean like Nacogdoches and Natchitoches?" We had to laugh at that. I guess he was right.

On May 13, 1864, the advance elements of the Yankee XV

Corps arrived from the north to find Johnston's strong position and the presence of Polk's reinforcements. Union General McPherson commanded the central brigade, General Schofield the western brigade, and our old enemy, General Thomas, commanded the eastern brigade.

On May 14, McPherson launched a full-scale frontal assault at our center. Schofield simultaneously moved to attack Polk's Division protecting the western flank of the ridge. The Yankees took the field in row upon row of blue uniforms and regimental flags. They filled the battlefield from west to east, completely covering the area between the two flanking rivers. As best as I could remember, it was the most Yankees I had ever seen at one time.

"Look at that, Noah. Ain't it a sight?"

"Looks like a right sight of trouble to me."

"See yonder on the west side. You can see that whole brigade breakin' off to take on Polk. He better be through prayin' and ready to fight."

While we spoke, the Confederate cannon began to fire solid shot at extreme range. We could see the track of the twelve pound shot through the air. As the iron cannonballs smashed into the tightly packed Union formations, they pierced through rank after rank of soldiers. As they struck human flesh, the bodies themselves became projectiles, spinning into their fellow soldiers on either side, killing even more men. Triangles of destruction showed where each strike occurred. But the blue lines reformed, stepping over the dead and dying, as the cannons continued to take their toll.

Finally, the Yankees broke out with a mighty yell and began to march forward on the double quick. Bugles sounded and they charged headlong at the defenses at the bottom of the hill. The aim of the cannon was adjusted and they were loaded with canister. The twelve pound loads of musket balls laid down Yankees like wheat before a mighty reaper. We added rifle fire with deadly effect. The blue tide shattered on the rock of our defenses.

General Johnston sent a corps swinging to the right. They smashed hard into the Union left flank and began rolling them up like a giant carpet. Stanley's Union division turned to fight, but General John Bell Hood, the battle scarred veteran from Texas, slowly drove them ever farther back. A large battery of artillery from the Fifth Indiana Regiment poured well aimed fire into Hood's Corp, slowing their progress. Federal reinforcements stopped the Confederate advance. Hood's men held their ground, refusing to retreat. They presented a deadly threat to the Union left flank. On the western flank, Schofield barreled into Polk's reinforced troops. Polk's men grudgingly gave way until they were under the protective guns of Hardee's Corps on the Ridge.

The night was mild and humid. We were allowed to leave the line by platoons to fix a hot supper. The fried bacon and cornbread went down good with the Yankee coffee. Unfortunately, we had run out of the borrowed sugar. We slept as well as we could in our blankets in the trenches. Anxious bugles awakened us in the morning to find the Yankees moving across the battlefield to strike the right flank of the ridge. The Confederate cannon pierced the morning air with solid shot aimed into the marching blue regiments.

Johnston ordered Hood to reengage the Union east flank, which he did with vigor. On our right, the Union succeeded in capturing the Cherokee Indian Volunteer's forward artillery battery at the base of the hill, but the supporting brigade of Cherokee Infantry drove back the Yankees and recaptured the guns. Federal General Sweeny managed to get a whole division of troops across the Oostanaula River on a pontoon bridge that had been constructed during the night on the left. His goal was to swing past Polk's troops and assault our supply train.

General Sherman had gathered all three of his columns together at Resaca. There were now one hundred and ten thousand Union troops, plus artillery and cavalry, at Resaca to oppose our fifty-four thousand Confederates. Through the day of May 15, we held off the much larger army. The Yankees were exhausted from the forced march and not yet organized into battle formation. After dark, Johnston extricated our army from Resaca and moved to keep the Confederate army between Sherman and Atlanta. Resaca was counted as a Confederate victory. We had resisted the North for two days and kept the smaller Confederate army together, plus we had again stopped the Yankees in their tracks. How long could we hold out against such a large army with all the supplies in the world? Bridges and railroads were destroyed to hold back the blue tide. But within days, the Federals had repaired the damage and relentlessly pursued the Army of Tennessee.

12

May, 1864, outskirts of Atlanta, Georgia

THE CONFEDERATES LED the Yankees in a deadly dance around Atlanta, and it was Johnston who called the tune. Each engagement kept the blue coats off balance and was designed to save the Army of Tennessee while bleeding the Yankee army. We played for time, hoping our opponent would make a fatal mistake. We could expect few reinforcements, and nothing short of a miracle would save Atlanta. Nothing short of a miracle could save the Confederacy.

We were still assigned to Hardee's Corps as part of Cleburne's Division, but our brigade had a new commander. Brigadier General Hiram Granbury, a Texan, was our new commander. He was the man for the job. He brought out the best our brigade had to offer. He was loved and respected by the men. For the rest of the war, we would proudly be known as Granbury's Brigade.

Our first battle under Granbury came May 17, 1864, at Adairsville, Georgia. General Howard, our old enemy from Chickamauga, and the Union IV Corps, were coming down the road hard and fast on Johnston's Army. He detailed Hardee's Corps to delay the Yankees long enough for the rest of the Army of Tennessee to get out of Howard's reach. Howard sent the Forty-fourth Illinois and the Twenty-fourth Wisconsin as a vanguard to knock us out of the way. We made a stand at Adairsville. Our line was centered around an unusual octagonal house belonging to Robert Saxon. I don't know what the Yankees were expecting, but they got all they wanted and then some. Fighting around the shelter of buildings and barns, we threw together some hasty shallow trenches reinforced with logs and fence rails. Many of our men had Spencer rifles. We were some of the best scavengers around. If there was something left on the battlefield by either a Yankee or Confederate soldier that we could use, we took it. We took rifles, pistols, cartridges, caps, coats and boots. We took blankets and food. We were always glad to find coffee, as we rarely had any, and got tired of scorched grain made into a poor substitute.

Three seasoned Confederate divisions, a total of nine regiments, awaited the two Yankee regiments. Their forward units scouted ahead and reported they were heavily outnumbered. I can only guess their reasons. Perhaps they didn't believe their scouts; maybe they thought we would break and run; maybe they thought their main body would arrive in time to sweep us away; maybe they were just overconfident. Whatever the reason, they attacked us.

They assembled to attack in a long line about four ranks deep. We had no artillery, but neither did the Yankees. They bravely charged forward with fixed bayonets. We poured well aimed rifle fire into their line beginning at about one hundred yards. Nine thousand rifles spat out a deadly barrage of bullets against the twenty-two hundred men. The bullets mowed them down. By the time the muzzle loading Enfield rifles were reloaded, the Yankees were at the deadly range of fifty yards. Our second volley killed hundreds more Billy Yanks. Those of us with repeating rifles poured all we had in the Union force. The assault staggered, then stopped. A third volley caused them to break and run. Hardee ordered a bayonet charge. We emerged from behind the houses and our makeshift trenches, screaming the Rebel yell. The Yankees ran so fast the dust didn't catch up to them.

Sergeant Howard sent us out to scavenge the field. We filled tow sack after tow sack of rifle and pistol cartridges. We found a couple more dozen Spencer rifles with an abundance of rim fire cartridges. We also came back with bacon and hard tack from the soldiers' war bags, and a little loose change. There were enough horses and mules that we needed plenty of help to butcher them. We had to hurry because the main body of the Union Army was pressing relentlessly forward. We got our horse meat and contraband and headed back to rejoin the main army. We took some of the choice loin cuts to General Cleburne and General Granbury. They gladly accepted it the fresh meat; even generals got tired of salt pork.

General Cleburne recognized me. "Well, Private Turner, my favorite Irish Texas soldier. This is Brigadier General Hiram Granbury, commander of your brigade. He's a Texan like you and me."

I snapped a sharp salute. "It's a pleasure, sir."

Granbury looked me up one side and down the other. "Son, how old are you?"

"Beggin' the General's pardon, sir, do you mean how old the army says I am, or how old my Momma says I am?"

He glanced at General Cleburne who had started laughing and grinning at me. "Your commanding officer is askin' you a question, Private Turner."

"According to the Confederate Army, I was fifteen when I enlisted, which means I'm seventeen now. I was born in 1850, sir, so I'm really only fourteen."

General Granbury gave me a second look. "That means you were only twelve when you enlisted. We do grow 'em big in Texas. Why did you want to enlist, son?"

"My two brothers and my brother-in-law enlisted. The recruiter kept sayin' how we would be marchin' on the road to glory. I didn't want to miss out, sir."

"Well, have you found the road to glory, Private Turner?"

"No disrespect, General, but most of the time, it seems more like we're goin' to hell in a hand basket, sir."

They sat back on their horses and laughed like I had said something really funny. General Cleburne asked me why I had come to see them.

"Well, General, one of my jobs is scavenging the battlefields. I butchered some fresh killed horses and brought the back straps to you. It's fresh and ought to be really good, sir."

They both laughed again. I just smiled, since I had no idea what was so funny. He motioned for an aide to come take the meat from me. "Aaron, thank you, son. That's about the nicest thing anybody has done for me in a long time. You best be gettin' back to your company now. Mary, Joseph and Patrick guard you, lad."

I felt like I was ten feet tall and bulletproof. These two great heroes knew my name and had shared a laugh with me. Being a courier had some advantages.

General Johnston positioned us to defend Altoona Pass, but Sherman flanked the whole Confederate army. Johnston swung the army to a place called New Hope Church. Sherman sent Hooker's Corps to pass through the small town, not realizing the whole Army of Tennessee waited there. We scorched that ol' rooster's tail feathers good that day.

The Payton brothers put up quite a spectacle. Corporal Harold Payton was a crack shot with a rifle. He had picked a good spot from which he could choose his shots. As soon as he fired, his brother, Bradley, handed him another loaded rifle. They had five rifles and kept them going. Harold was picking off the officers and sergeants. When their officers were dead, the men didn't know what to do and began to fall back, colliding with the units behind them, creating chaos. The two of them together accounted for seven officers, four sergeants and five enlisted men. The rest of us took advantage of the confusion to pour a hot fire into the Yankees, finally driving them from the field.

Johnston captured thirty-four supply wagons that day loaded

with cartridges, clothes, blankets, tents, food and medicine. They shared them out evenly. Lieutenant Kinney sent us scavenging again. His son, Trent, went with us. The dead Yankees had full cartridge pouches and coat pockets. We loaded up with blankets, jackets, shoes and boots. We found a few more Spencer rifles and some canisters of cartridges. We picked up another Colt .44 with a belt, holster, and a full cartridge pouch. Some Yankees carried their bed rolls across their chests like we did, and others used knapsacks. We could always use extra blankets and bedding tarps. Some of the knapsacks had clothes we could use, paper and pencils, sulphur matches, playing cards, coffee, sugar and salt. Trent found a pair of false teeth we took back for a joke. He liked to have scared Dane Carthel to death with them. Some of the Yankees had small change in their pockets and a little folding money. That day I picked up $87.42. I didn't feel a bit bad about taking it. Those men sure weren't going to need it. There were six dead horses we butchered. We saved the green hides to make various repairs, especially on our shoes. They didn't last as long as cow hides, but it sure beat going bare foot.

13

May, 1864, Pickett's Mill, Georgia

JOHNSTON'S ARMY SKIRM-
ished with the Yankees at Dallas and Pumpkin Vine Creek,
but only long enough to slow them down. He set the Army
in a good defensive position at Picket's Mill, Georgia. We
dug trenches topped with logs. Hardee's Corps anchored
the right end of the line. Cleburne's Division was on the
far right end. Granbury's Brigade anchored the end of
Cleburne's line, so we were the far right end of the whole
line. We were tucked back at an angle from the main line
to keep the Yankees from turning the flank.

Sherman started the dance by sending the whole
Union IV Corps against Cleburne's Division. The Yankees
had to cross open ground to get to the earthworks in front
of Cleburne's Division. Our artillery opened up on them.
The grape and canister worked death and misery on them,
but they kept coming, hardly slowing down.

They fixed bayonets and came at a full charge
straight at our lines. Our boys in gray gave as good as
they got, and the line held. The Yankees regrouped and
tried again, shifting a little farther to the right. They hit
the place where Govan's Arkansas Brigade was waiting.
I don't know what anybody else thinks of those wild

men from Arkansas, but they sure can fight. They finally drove the Federals off. The dead Yankees were stacked up like cordwood in front of Govan's part of the line.

The Yankees tried again. This time they swung even farther to our right flank. As they crossed the field in front of Cleburne's Division, the artillery tore gaping holes in their lines that were immediately filled up by more blue uniforms. Soon, they were in formation in front of our end of the line.

Captain Tyus signaled for me. "Aaron, you ride like the devil to find General Granbury. Tell him we're in too deep and need help, and we need it fast."

I kicked my heels back hard into the little bay horse and rode like the wind. I saw General Granbury with his staff close by.

"Captain Tyus' compliments, sir."

"You're the one who brought me the horse steaks. They were excellent. What can I do for you, Private Turner?"

I grinned that he remembered my name, but the heavy rifle fire behind me reminded me of the seriousness of my message. "Captain Tyus says we're in deep and need immediate heavy reinforcement, sir."

"Yes. Captain Tyus isn't one to ask for help if he doesn't need it. Son, I don't have any reserves to send, but General Cleburne is holding some reserves. Ride to him and tell him General Granbury's right flank needs immediate support."

I rode the bay for all he was worth until I saw General Cleburne and his staff directing the defense along the whole right of the line. The Yankees were pushing there, too.

"General Granbury's compliments, sir."

"Yes. Well, it's Private Turner from Texas. What can I do for General Granbury?"

"Sir, his brigade is in over its head and in need of immediate reinforcement."

"Son, do you know how many troops are opposing Granbury's Brigade?"

"Three Yankee brigades, sir."

"That's pretty tough odds even for Texas soldiers. Major Ford, take the First, Fifty-fourth and Fifty-seventh Georgia regiments to reinforce Granbury. Get 'em there fast, Major. I'll hold the Sixty-third Georgia in reserve."

"Aaron, you tell Granbury help is on the way. Ride, son, ride!"

The horse slid to a stop nearer to General Granbury than I intended, drawing a reprimand from a gray bearded major. "Sorry, sir. General Cleburne's compliments. He is sendin' the First, Fifty-fourth, and Fifty-seventh Georgia Infantry under Major Ford. They are headin' this way on the double, sir."

"Thank you, Private. Take the news back to Captain Tyus, then report to your platoon. We need every gun on the line. You staff officers, grab some rifles and follow me. We're going to kill a few Yankees, too."

I knew it was a desperate situation when staff officers and generals fought in the trenches with rifles and bayonets. I reported to Captain Tyus. He looked more worried than I had ever seen him. He had discarded his sword for a rifle, bayonet, and a pistol. He just waved me on toward my platoon.

I was almost back to my platoon when my horse stumbled and squealed in pain. Blood was pouring from a bullet wound in his left shoulder. I pulled my Spencer from the scabbard just before he rolled over and died. I gathered my canister of rifle magazines and all my cartridges for my revolver. I ran to Lieutenant Kinney and told him help was coming. His face was black with powder smoke and his uniform splattered with blood. He pointed to his right and waved with his pistol.

I found myself in the trench next to Trent Kinney, Quartermaster Sergeant Matthews, Sergeant Howard and his boys. I picked my shots with my Spencer and began firing as fast as I could aim and pull the trigger. Our company had quite a few Spencers scattered up and down the line. This increased our rate of fire. But even so, the sheer number of Yankees was about to overwhelm our brigade.

As I was changing out an empty magazine, a blue uniform loomed over the log at the top of the trench. He lunged at me, burying his bayonet to the hilt in the wool fabric in the left side of my coat. He jerked unsuccessfully to free his bayonet so he could kill me. I tried to get loose to defend myself. Seeing the danger I was in, Quartermaster Sergeant Matthews sliced him across the belly with his bayonet. The Yankee screamed in agony as his intestines spilled forward, covering me in blood and gore. His body landed on top of me, trapping me under the screaming, dying man. Trent smashed him in the head with the butt of his rifle, putting the poor man out of his misery. I tried to get up, but my feet were tangled in his intestines and I fell.

When I finally got to my feet, a Yankee jumped into the trench and knocked me back hard with the barrel of his rifle. I staggered backwards into the wall of the trench as he lunged at me with his bayonet. I pulled my LeMatt from the holster, and fired a load of buckshot into the man's bearded face. Blood and brains splattered my face and coat.

Sergeant Matthews was shot in the chest at close range. He slumped back dead next to me in the trench. I never got to thank him for saving my life. A Yankee slashed at Trent with his bayonet. I shot him at point blank range in the ribs with my LeMatt. The .44 caliber ball opened a fist sized hole in his chest, killing him instantly.

Two Yankees sprang in the trench. They came screaming at me with their bayonets. Skeet Howard saw them coming and ran to help. He shot one dead with his rifle, then broke the collar bone of the other Yankee with his rifle butt. With a fierce, wild look in his eyes, Skeet finished the injured man with his bayonet. We heard the trample of many feet behind us. The Georgia boys had arrived and were lined up three ranks deep behind our trench.

"Front rank, fire! Second rank, fire! Third rank, fire!"

The noise of their rifles above our heads was deafening. I covered my ears with my hands. I could feel the hot wave of burned powder rush by each time they fired. The Yankees turned and ran from the withering fire. The Georgians crowded into the trench with us until we were shoulder to shoulder. The Yankees tried one more assault, but the reinforced line was too much. Their charge faltered.

A bugle sounded as a small regiment of Louisiana cavalry

charged around the end of the line and took the Yankee assault in the flank. The sudden appearance of the cavalry drove the Federals from the field and broke their attack on our end of the line. The Louisiana cavalry regrouped and charged into the rear of the retreating Union troops. This caused a confused panic. The Yankees ran across the battlefield, exposing themselves to rifle fire from the line. All along the front of Cleburne's Division, .50 caliber lead balls slammed into the running soldiers. The Union assault at Pickett's Mill was over. We had won another battle by the skin of our teeth. Had it not been for the arrival of the Georgia boys, our line could not have held out much longer. It had been a close run thing.

————

Sergeant Howard came along after the fight. He had Dane Carthel, Ky and Ham with him to drag away the dead bodies. He found me sitting on the edge of the trench where I had fought. Even though it was hot, I was shivering. Scalding tears washed streaks in the powder and blood stains on my face. He sat down next to me. His face was black with powder, and his jacket was stiff with blood.

"Aaron, you had a pretty rough day today. Take a swallow from this canteen and wash the powder out of your mouth, then have a good long drink. You look like you could use it. I saw that horse get shot out from under you. You're the one that brought them Georgia boys over here. I seen you take out a few of them Billy Yanks, too. I reckon you done better than most growed men. I'm real proud to have you in my platoon. If I had a hundred like you, I think we could chase Sherman all the way back to hide under his momma's bed. I seen Pink and Noah down the line. They're alright. When you think you're up to it, I'm gonna send you out to scavenge again; seems like you always find the good stuff."

I looked up at him as I wiped the tears off my face and blew my nose on a bloody sleeve. I tried to talk, but the best I could manage was to croak out a hoarse "Thanks."

That evening, Generals Granbury and Cleburne rode by our battered brigade. General Granbury was leading a sorrel horse. Our officers ordered us to attention. Those who were able stood up and saluted. Even many of the wounded managed to salute. Captain Tyus, smoke and blood stained, leaning on a rifle and bayonet, gave a sharp salute. He looked like he had been run over by a herd of buffalo.

General Granbury returned the salute and asked where he could find Private Turner, the courier. Captain Tyus turned and pointed me out along the line. I was covered in powder smoke, blood and a little vomit. "Well, Private Turner, do you know you are responsible for all government property entrusted in your care by the Confederacy?"

"Sir?"

"I saw a Confederate horse shot out from under you today. Is that correct, Private?"

I trembled as I responded "Yes, sir, that nice little bay gelding."

"Well, you seem like a good young man, bein' from Texas an' all. I'd hate to see you gettin' in any trouble. One of my aides caught this Yankee horse runnin' loose on the battle field. You see that US branded on his hip?"

"Sir?"

"This is a replacement horse to keep you out of trouble with Jefferson Davis."

The men in the company began to laugh. It was only then that I realized he was rewarding me.

"You bring General Cleburne and me some more horse or mule steaks once in a while, and we'll call it even."

"Yes, sir, General Granbury!"

While the group of officers were still assembled there, a body of elegantly uniformed high ranking Confederate officers rode up to join Cleburne and Granbury. They quickly saluted. It was General Joseph Johnston himself.

"General Cleburne, I have turned to your division again and again. They have always given their best. Today, General Granbury's Brigade, an important part of your division, distinguished themselves. They fought with courage and determination that is rarely seen. They held out against staggering odds and repeated attacks in defense of the right wing of the entire Army of Tennessee. Had they failed, we would likely have suffered a terrible defeat today. Because of their stubborn bravery, we won a great victory. As of today, I designate them as General Joseph Johnston's personal Brigade of Honor." He and his staff drew their sabers with a flourish and saluted Generals Cleburne and Granbury, then turned their horses and saluted the troops on the line.

We stood momentarily in stunned silence. Then wild cheering broke out all up and down the line of Granbury's Brigade. I was too hoarse to cheer. I just held the reins of the sorrel horse and began to cry tears of joy and emotion mixed with anguish. My friends Wade Riley, Monty McNeal and Taylor Edwards died there that day, as did Sergeant Matthews, who had saved my life. Of the original thirty-four members of our platoon who had left Texas in 1862, only nineteen were left alive.

14

June 1864, Atlanta, Georgia

I HAD ALWAYS THOUGHT summer along the Navasota River in Texas was about as hot and humid as a boy could stand. I was wrong. Georgia in June is worse, a lot worse. Heat lay across the land like a thick damp blanket. The air was usually heavy and still. When there was a breeze, it brought no relief. The nights were almost as bad as the days. I would lie on top of my blankets in just my cotton drawers and sweat all night. Noah and I went back into the "Miracle Mosquito Salve" business, but since no one had any money to buy it, we just gave it away. At least we had plenty of supplies with the Union army so close all the time.

"Noah, I bet the corn ought to be up about knee high by now and the cotton off to a good start."

"Bet you're right. We'd be runnin' the cultivator and gettin' ready to start hoein'. I'd rather be home with a hoe than here with a rifle and a bunch of Yankees tryin' to kill us."

"I'm sure missin' Mary Ann, too." Pink complained.

Johnston had kept us moving to keep the Federal army off balance and away from Atlanta and the railroads. There were enough Yankees around Atlanta that if they had combined their forces and pinned us down, they could have whipped us once and for all. But General Johnston was good at pushing forward or pulling back at just the right time and place to give us a fighting chance of taking on any one part of Sherman's army at a time. That was the best we could hope for.

We worked our way around until we were northwest of Atlanta on Kennesaw Mountain. The army had dug trenches and shored them up with logs. Our artillery was carefully placed. If the Yankees wanted Atlanta, they would have to deal with our position on Kennesaw Mountain; it would be too dangerous to leave a force of our size loose behind them.

Toward the end of June the Yankees were forming up for an attack against our position. On the morning of June 27, 1864, bugles sounded up and down the Union lines. Thousands of soldiers in blue were on the move. Once they were in range, our artillery opened up on them. They finally charged, driving our skirmishers back into the rifle pits at the base of the mountain. The bruised and battered Army of Tennessee turned the Yankees back, charge after charge. Finally, the surging blue wave broke through the front lines. The soldiers from the rifle pits at the base of the mountain were mostly able to escape to the second line of defense. The trenches were so packed with men that they were able to mow the Yankees down like hay in a meadow. After trying all day, the Yankees retreated the way they had come.

We did our usual scavenging after the battle and found plenty of things we needed. But we got something we didn't expect that would affect us for the rest of the war. General Joe Johnston was replaced as our commander by General John Bell Hood. We all thought "Uncle Joe" was the best commander we had ever known.

We didn't know that much about Hood, except for the few months that he had been a corps commander since the Battle of Resaca. We did know that he was not Joe Johnston, and that was a powerful strike against him. He was known throughout the Confederacy as a man of great personal valor. He had lost an arm and a leg as a corps commander under General Lee. Most men would have been satisfied that they had given their all and gone home. General John Bell Hood had straps built to hold him in the saddle while he soldiered on. Lee considered Hood's Brigade the finest troops in his command. He claimed "The Texans always move them."

While waiting for a message, I had listened to a conversation between Generals Cleburne and Granbury. Johnston's departure had something to do with politics. He had angered President Davis, while General Hood was a favorite of the President. General Cleburne said he feared Hood was too much wolf and not enough fox, that he was aggressive to the point of recklessness. Granbury responded that while Johnston was a fencing master, Hood was the master of the battle axe. Only later would I fully realize the truth of that statement.

———

On July 20, 1864, at Peach Tree Creek, we got our first real taste of Hood's aggressive style of command. The Yankees were attempting to cross the creek at three widely separated fords. Hood saw a chance to attack while the Union forces were temporarily divided. He ordered a full scale frontal assault at the corps commanded by General Thomas.

The Yankees reeled back from the attack and were hotly pursued. However, Thomas was no fool and organized a fighting retreat to the rolling hills north of the once peaceful creek. The Union skillfully turned to fight, taking up defensive positions. They formed deep orderly ranks of rifles which poured a deadly, continuous fire into our advancing troops.

The next Union corps to the west came to reinforce Thomas and hit the strung out Confederates hard and fast in the flank. Hood's forces were forced to retreat with heavy losses. Almost five thousand Confederate soldiers lay dead or wounded along Peach Tree Creek out of a force of forty-four thousand.

On July 22, 1864, Hood had the army arranged in a good defensive position with an outer perimeter of rifle pits and a strong second line some distance back. He hoped to entice Union General McPherson to send his corps to attack. Hood had our troops abandon the outer line so the Federals might be tempted to attack the apparently retreating army. This might have worked, but he reached too far. He dispatched Hardee's Corps, a full third of the Army of Tennessee, off to attack Sherman's exposed supply train east of Atlanta.

General Hardee passed the orders down the chain of command. I delivered the orders to General Cleburne, General Granbury, regimental commander Colonel Smith, Captain Tyus and Lieutenant Kinney. I didn't like what I saw. They each reacted with a look of deep concern and then signed the written order.

Lieutenant Kinney explained to our company that we were to make a forced march of fifteen miles to the east, then hit Sherman's lightly guarded supply wagons. Hood hoped this would draw some of the troops away from the main fight to defend the supplies. We rolled our blankets, filled our canteens, loaded our cartridge pouches, and stuffed food in our pockets.

The July heat was oppressive as we pushed hard through the countryside. We had left camp at dawn and reached the supply train of hundreds of wagons by early afternoon. Wheeler's good Rebel cavalry had screened our march, but the dust of fourteen thousand men marching in July is hard to conceal.

The Yankees had seen our movement and guessed our destination. McPherson began diverting troops and alerted General Sherman. Seeing the Union army stretching away to the east to catch Hardee's Corps, Hood ordered Cheatham's Corps to attack them in the flank.

Cheatham's concentrated force broke the Union advance and sent them into an orderly retreat. Sherman himself took command of his crumbling center. His men turned to fight. A heavy battery was wheeled into place on a knoll that swept General Cheatham's position. Cheatham doggedly attacked the reformed Union center. By four in the afternoon, Chatham's Corp was spent. He organized them into a fighting retreat. The Yankees, too tired to pursue, allowed them to leave the battlefield. Eight thousand Confederate soldiers lay dead and dying.

Those of us in Hardee's Corps enjoyed some success on the east by capturing the supply train and driving away the escorting troops. We left the plunder under heavy guard and attacked the exposed Union flank. At first the exposed end of the Union line collapsed upon itself. Their officers quickly regrouped them for a fighting retreat. Our early success was short-lived as heavy Federal reinforcements arrived and stopped our progress. We had gained an enormous amount of supplies, but at a staggering cost in lives that could not be replaced.

The next day Hood launched our exhausted army against the Union Corps under our old nemesis, General Howard, at Ezra Church. Our troops were driven back with heavy losses. In the days since Hood had taken command, fully a third of our army was gone. In twenty-three days, eighteen thousand of our total fifty-four thousand brave young soldiers had been lost: too much wolf, not enough fox.

The Union objective was to gradually work their way around Atlanta to the west to cut off the railroads which were the only source of resupply from the west. The Yankees already controlled the Western and Atlantic Railroad from Chattanooga to the outskirts of Atlanta. They received supplies regularly. Steamboats shipped huge amounts of war materials to Chattanooga where they were loaded onto trains and sent to Atlanta. Confederate cavalry patrols disrupted some train shipments, but most were sent heavily guarded by infantry on the trains. The Georgia Line connected Atlanta to the blockaded port of Savannah. Only a few men and a minor amount of materials came to Atlanta that way. The Macon and Western

Railroad ran south to Macon then on into Florida. This line was open and could ship anything they had to send which was almost nothing. Some fresh vegetables, food, and a handful of men arrived in Atlanta, but little else. The big prize was the Atlanta and West Point Railroad which stretched far away into the deep south. The bulk of the men and materials that reached Atlanta came in on this line.

On August 2, General Schofield's Army of the Ohio moved from the Union left flank behind the cover of the rest of the Federal lines, in a long sweeping arc, all the way to the Union right flank. Schofield hesitated on the north bank of Utoy Creek waiting for his supply train to catch up with his men. Hood seized the opportunity to shift his forces into position. On August 5, the Yankees were vulnerable as they crossed the creek. When half of Schofield's men were on either side of the creek, Hood unleashed a vicious attack. Schofield's Army was routed with heavy Union losses. It was the first taste of victory we had known since Pickett's Mill. This round went to the wolf. I had been kept occupied as a courier in the last few battles and had not fired a shot since that terrible day.

15

August 20, 1864, Lovejoy's Station,
south of Atlanta

THE YANKEES SENT A HUGE
cavalry raid to Lovejoy's Station. They had scattered
the small detachment guarding the train station and
had torn up the tracks to keep the trains from getting
through. They swarmed in like locust the next day to hit
the supply depot at Jonesborough. They swept aside the
small garrison, destroying huge amounts of irreplaceable
clothes, food, and ammunition stored there.

On August 20, 1864, Hood ordered Cleburne's
Division to Lovejoy's Station. We had to march across
Atlanta from the northeastern edge where we had been
camped to the station which was more or less due south
of the city. We arrived just as the sun was setting. The
Yankee troopers were dismounted and tending their
horses as they picketed them for the night.

General Cleburne immediately recognized the
vulnerable position of the unsuspecting Union cavalry.
He immediately had us form up to attack. With the purple
sky of twilight in the west, we raised the Rebel yell and fell
upon them like wolves among sheep. We swept the few
Yankee skirmishers from the field and hit the Yankees like

a hammer on hot iron. I fired my Spencer as fast as I could work the lever and reload. The Federals tried to form a defensive line, but we were on them too soon. They ran for their lives, leaving their horses behind. We chased them and shot them down like rabbits until we were too tired to continue. It was a complete victory. Hundreds of good quality horses, repeating rifles, and tons of desperately needed supplies were captured. The Yankees had found no love or joy at Lovejoy's Station. It was the last taste of victory we would know for the rest of the war.

On August 31, a large body of Federal troops was observed moving back into Jonesborough. Cleburne's Division was still near Lovejoy's Station available to respond. No one knew how many Yankees were coming. Hood deployed Cleburne's Division to hold things together while he sent reinforcements. Hood didn't know what to expect, but sent two full corps to reinforce Cleburne. What Hood did not know was that Sherman had stripped his whole line to a skeleton defense. Of his total seven corps, he sent six to Jonesborough. Before the battle began, Hood had second thoughts about the security of Atlanta, so he recalled one of the two corps, leaving Hardee's Corps to fight six Federal corps alone.

It wasn't much of a battle. General Hardee realized we were completely overmatched. He organized a fighting retreat to the defenses at Lovejoy's Station. He sent me with an urgent message to General Hood.

I rode my sorrel Yankee horse like my life depended on it. I found Hood and his staff, but dared not approach him myself, so I found an aide.

"General Hardee's compliments, sir. I have an urgent dispatch for General Hood."

"Doesn't everybody? Hand it over!" He opened the canvas cover and pulled out the note written on paper inside. "My God!

General Hood, sir! General! Hardee's Corp is facing six full Federal corps, sir!"

Hood looked momentarily confused, then responded grimly. General Hardee was to attempt to retreat in an orderly fashion to the southwest. The remainder of the Army of Tennessee would depart Atlanta and join Hardee's Corps somewhere to the southwest. The Confederate Army was abandoning Atlanta.

The Yankees chased us completely out of Lovejoy's Station, then stopped. Their mission had been accomplished. The whole sky over Atlanta was thick with billowing smoke as the last of Hood's soldiers burned anything of military value. Tremendous explosions rocked the smoke stained sky as ammunition depots were destroyed. As night fell, the whole city of Atlanta was on fire. An orange and yellow glow reflected from the thick smoke. With the fall of Atlanta, the defeat of the South was inevitable. Perhaps it had always been inevitable. I watched the flames lick high into the smoke thickened night sky and listened to the unceasing explosions. The road to glory had led me to the open gates of a burning hell. I wanted to go home.

16

September 2, 1864, western Georgia

WE MARCHED. WE MARCHED day after day and into the night. We marched with slumped shoulders and broken spirits. We marched away from Atlanta, away from Sherman and his army. We marched into western Georgia and into northern Alabama. We marched in the rain and mud, we marched in stifling heat and choking dust. We marched in defeated silence.

We had left most of our belongings behind us, because we had run for our lives. We had been defeated before and retreated. This time we had been routed and run from the battlefield as fast as we could run. My sorrel horse had been left behind. Jake Wade, who was our company comedian tried to cheer us up, but his jokes rang hollow and didn't hide the sadness in his own voice. The Hunters had lost all their instruments except for the Irish flute which had been in Justin's hip pocket. We were a funeral procession of twenty-four thousand men marching to a silent funeral dirge. Our hopes had died with the fall of Atlanta. It was just a matter of time before the whole Confederacy would die a slow bloody death, but not before sacrificing the lives of many more men. Forty-four thousand Confederate soldiers had marched to the defense of Atlanta. Only twenty-four thousand were left to run away.

General Hood hoped to get behind Sherman and cut his supply lines. If he succeeded, Sherman might delay his descent upon Savannah, or detach troops to deal with Hood's remnant of an army. We tore up tracks, burned bridges, and destroyed water stations along the railroad. We pulled up track, built fires with the cross ties and bent the great steel rails until they could never be used again. Our two weeks of destruction complete, we ducked into northern Alabama to wait for the Yankees to take the bait.

The Yankees came alright. They backed trains all the way from Atlanta with hundreds of flat cars loaded with new rails and cross ties. The trains carried equipment to lay the tracks in record time. They brought engineers to direct the rebuilding of the railroads and bridges. They delivered thousands of men to work and fifty thousand more to protect them. What took us weeks to destroy took the Federals just days to rebuild better than before. The trains rolled unhindered from Atlanta to Chattanooga and back carrying the war materials of an unbeatable foe.

It seemed that the fortunes of war had abandoned us. I was hungry, tired and discouraged. At every turn another misfortune awaited our tattered shadow of an army. Hood's whole Army couldn't muster twenty-four thousand men, counting those walking wounded and those who were too sick to fight, but who limped along with the army. Cleburne's fabled division was combined with three other divisions to reach just half strength. The Texas Fifteenth Regiment and Company F both had less than half the number who had so proudly left Texas in 1862.

Even nature itself increased our misery. One night along the march, a tremendous thunderstorm exploded across the mountains. The wind rose higher until it screamed above us. A giant tree snapped like a twig in the wind. It fell across a huddled group of men in our regiment killing one and injuring eight. Days later, the night sky poured out its wrath. As we camped high on a ridge, another terrible lightning storm shattered the mountain air. A blinding flash exploded like an artillery shell in the middle of our camp. One man was burned to death and others were injured from being thrown around like toys. It left me night-blind with ringing in my ears until the morning.

Our rations were nothing more than parched corn three times a day, and not too much of that. We stretched our diet a little if one of the few remaining horses or mules died, but there wasn't much to go around. There was no game to be found. We searched for hickory nuts, but it was too early in the fall. We might find a handful of muscadine grapes or some late black berries. It was too early for the persimmons to be ripe. Passing armies had cleaned everything else out, and most of the farms in the area had been abandoned.

We camped near Tuscumbia, Alabama, on the Tennessee River. Our engineers were building a pontoon bridge across the river. The Tennessee was so wide at this point, that it was necessary to build a bridge to an island in the middle of the river, then build a second span the rest of the way across.

We received a large shipment of new clothes and shoes. I had been barefoot for a few weeks. My feet had grown a lot and I had been unable to scavenge any shoes or boots that fit. I sure was glad to get these.

"Baby brother-in-law, come over here. Let me see how tall you've gotten. You, too, Noah."

Pink had us stand back to back in our bare feet. Noah was still about two inches taller than me. "Close as I can guess, Noah, you're about six foot three inches. Aaron, looks like you're every bit of six foot one. And both of you look like bean poles. Noah's 'Arks' are about the biggest feet I ever seen, and Aaron, your feet ain't far behind."

Pink's measuring had attracted a little crowd from the platoon. Soon, Jamison and Justin Hunter were standing back to back. Justin still had him beat by a few inches, but he lacked three inches catching big brothers Jordan and Jonathan. Jake Ward had already passed his big brother, TJ, by several inches, and was closing in fast on his cousin, Pecos. Trent Kinney was now taller than his daddy. In the two years since we had left home some of us had grown taller and all had grown up hard and fast. There wasn't a boy among us, although there were many who were very young. The bloodstains of battle had changed all of us into hardened men who could look death in the eye without blinking.

We did a little unauthorized scavenging. There was a well-to-do farmer near where we camped. He had large corn fields drying down to harvest. He had cattle and mules and fine horses. He also had several large sturdy rail pens for hogs located quite a distance from his house to avoid the smell of the pigs. We hadn't had a taste of meat in six weeks. A few of us decided the farmer was going to make an involuntary contribution for the good of the cause.

Pecos, Jake and TJ Wade, John Stone, Dane Carthel, Noah and I formulated a tidy little plan. There had been rumors of Yankee cavalry patrols in the area looking for us and doing some scavenging themselves, plus some Union deserters, too. We had strict orders from General Hood not to bother any of the good Southern farmers or their belongings. We could, however, keep and use any "contraband" we found, meaning anything the Yankees had that we needed. John, TJ and Pecos climbed into the pens with the hogs. They roped the hogs by the back feet, while Dane, Noah, Jake and I ran up and slit their throats. We only wanted to take what we could use in Company F before it would spoil. With the warm weather, that would be about two days for the meat to turn bad; ten hogs ought to do it. We slipped the ropes under the bottom rail and silently dragged each hog off into the edge of the thick woods north of the hog pens. Once we had them there, we quickly field dressed them, leaving the head and entrails behind.

As we were doing this, we stumbled on something in the underbrush that clanked like crockery. Jake pulled the cork on one of the gallon jugs and immediately took a long hard swallow.

"Corn liquor, and it's pretty good, too. Looks like the ol' farmer has been sellin' some of his corn by the gallon. There's over twenty jugs here!"

We immediately gathered around Jake, who was taking a second sample, and each had a swallow. Jake's definition of pretty good didn't match mine, but I didn't complain. We loaded the hogs and jugs on our backs and made two trips to get it all back to camp. We might have made it back unnoticed into camp except for Jake. He had been sampling the same jug between trips and was in a high mood, singing loud and off key. Lieutenant Kinney came out to see what all the racket was about.

John spoke up for us. "Evenin', Lieutenant. We was just comin' to see you. We was out scoutin' for somethin' to eat when we come up on some Yankee deserters who had just butchered these here hogs. They ran like rabbits when they seen us and left all this fresh pork. And they had stole some whiskey somewhere, so we confiscated it. Best I understand it, all this stuff is contraband and fine for us to keep. We got some for you, too, sir."

Lieutenant Kinney grinned at John. "That was the way it was, Big John?"

"Well, pretty near, sir."

"Share it out to the whole company. Aaron, I've still got a horse. I believe Captain Tyus is visitin' General Granbury. I'm sure they would enjoy a hind quarter and a jug. Would you ride it up there to them?"

"Yes sir!"

I soon had the Lieutenant's horse saddled, and a gallon of corn liquor on one side of the horn and a nice hindquarter on the other. It seems that Captain Tyus and General Granbury were visiting with General Cleburne. "Private Turner, Texas Fifteenth, Company F, beggin' the officers' pardon for disturbin' you gentlemen."

"Well, my favorite Irish soldier from Texas. This lad belongs to your brigade, doesn't he Granbury? And your company, Captain Tyus? How can we be of assistance to you, Private Turner?"

"I brung y'all a fresh hindquarter of hog meat and a gallon jug of whiskey, sir."

"Did you, by thunder? And just how did you come on these great blessings, son?"

"Well, a few of us boys was out lookin' for somethin' to eat when we walked up on these Yankee deserters. They seen us and ran off and left all this nice fresh hog meat. And they musta stole some corn whiskey somewhere 'cause we found over twenty jugs. Since it was stolen goods, that makes it contraband so we can keep it, don't it, sir? We wanted to share with our officers, sir."

"How convenient of those Yankee deserters to leave all this behind. We'll enjoy the ham and the corn squeezin's, son. Oh, Aaron, before you go back to your unit, you might want to go down to the creek and wash the blood off your sleeves from butcherin' those hogs, just in case the farmer comes to camp."

I galloped back to our company. I could smell the pork cooking. We fried it in skillets and roasted it on sticks. We ate fresh pork until we were stuffed. The jugs had been making their way around too, putting everyone in a better mood. The Hunter's didn't have their guitar or fiddle, but Justin had his flute and Jonathan beat the time on an empty wooden case. The other brothers danced and sang. Jamison was dancing and singing with more than usual enthusiasm, and was really raising the dust. That is, until his father caught him in the jug. We clapped and sang with them. It was the first time I remembered being happy since Atlanta. Lulled to sleep by a full stomach and the warmth of the corn whiskey, I slept well that night and dreamed of home.

The pontoon bridge was finally finished. It was a grand thing to behold. We were proud of our engineers and what they had done. I sensed a little pride slipping quietly back into our lives. We marched across the mighty river into Tennessee on November 21, 1864. We made camp on the bluffs above the river. That night, the wind shifted to the north and blew with increasing fury all night long. The temperature dropped like a rock down a deep well. We built up the fires and put on the new overcoats we had received in Tuscumbia. Fat snowflakes fell thickly and began to stick to everything. By daylight, six inches of snow was on the ground and more, smaller, flakes were carried on the north wind. We broke camp and trudged on in the cold wind and snow until we reached Waynesboro, Tennessee.

The temperature continued to drop, but the snow stopped and the wind lessened. The water in our canteens froze, so we had to slowly melt the ice to have something to drink at supper. I sure was glad for the new woolen drawers and socks we had been supplied. We had good blankets and pieces of canvas for bedrolls, but we lacked tents. We found places where rocks or logs blocked the wind and managed to survive.

That day we received a very welcome reinforcement. Major General Nathan Bedford Forrest and his cavalry rode through the snow into our camp. One of his brigades was commanded by a sure enough real live Texas hero, Brigadier General Lawrence Sullivan Ross, or as we called him in Texas, Sul Ross. He had been an Indian fighter and Ranger back in Texas, and every boy in the state knew who he was. The cavalry had been sent to form the vanguard of our small army, scout out the enemy, and protect our flanks. Just knowing Sul Ross was there made me feel better.

We marched through the snow-clogged roads to Henryville, and made it to Mount Pleasant by the next night. Outside of Mount Pleasant, Ross's Cavalry chased off a large Union cavalry patrol. If there had been any doubt before, the Yankees now knew for sure we were coming. The next day outside of Campbellsville, Ross's Cavalry again skirmished with a large detachment of Union cavalry and captured sixty-five head of Yankee beef cattle and a supply wagon train. The wagons held blankets, coats, a few tents, rolls of canvas, foods, sugar and real coffee. The cattle were divided among Hood's twenty-four thousand men. None of us had a lot, but it sure was nice to get a meal of beef and have coffee and sugar.

The next morning, November 26, 1864, the cavalry skirmished

with Yankee infantry outside of Columbia. We were finally in contact with the Union army. General Schofield, who I learned from the officers, had been General Hood's roommate at West Point, had twenty thousand men from the Army of the Cumberland at Columbia camped along the south bank of the Duck River. They intended to get to Nashville to reinforce the Union troops there before the Rebs showed up to spoil their party. Hood had our infantry within three miles of Columbia by November 27. Schofield had collected his forces, crossed the Duck River and entered the defenses of Columbia. If he could bring Schofield to battle before they reached Nashville, we had a good chance of whipping them and then taking Nashville.

General Hood left two divisions of General S. D. Stephen's Corps and the artillery to assault Columbia. He took the rest of the army east with the intention of falling on Columbia from the rear. He sent those of us in Cleburne's Division up the turnpike to Davis Ford five miles above Columbia. The Governor of Tennessee, Isham Harris, and General Hood rode along with General Cleburne. The road north of Davis Ford was narrow and winding. Sixteen thousand men headed north in columns only four men wide. It was a slow and tedious process. The column snaked back over miles of road. We were extremely vulnerable to attack in this situation. We were to regroup at Spring Hill, north of Columbia, to fall on the rear of the Federal position.

General Schofield was no beginner. His scouts detected our movement. He began moving his troops out of Columbia and up the road to Spring Hill. He left enough men in Columbia to keep the two Confederate divisions there busy and to cover his troop movements. The majority of Schofield's army was already in Spring Hill by the time Cleburne's advance forces arrived. General Cleburne recognized that the Federal forces had just arrived and were road weary and disorganized. He sent three brigades to attack the Yankees before they established their defensive position. Lowery's Alabama Brigade formed the left wing of the attack. Our old friends in Govan's Arkansas Brigade were assigned the center. The Fifteenth Texas

Regiment was a proud part of Granbury's Brigade. We were to form the right wing.

As the rest of Cleburne's troops were moving into position, Lowery's Brigade was hit with the concentrated fire of a battery of eighteen Federal cannon. Lowery turned his men to face the cannon, but Federal reinforcements arrived to protect the battery before Lowery could attack.

The Yankees had two twelve pounders up the line that were tearing into Govan's troops. Cleburne redirected Granbury's Brigade to take the two gun battery. General Granbury gave the order for the Texas Fifteenth Regiment to charge. Three hundred angry Texans, all that survived of the entire original regiment of eleven hundred men, raised the Rebel yell, and charged straight for the Union guns and the supporting troops. The yell raised the wolf within my throat. My hands clenched my rifle tightly as we charged. The Union troops retreated so quickly they left the cannon on the field.

Things became confused when Hood sent other divisions to support the escalating conflict. The battle lines snaked crazily across the countryside. The Yankees also threw more troops into the confused fight. General Hood's orders were not clearly understood and seemed to be contradictory. The battlefield became a tangled mass of fighting men. Regiments became detached from their brigades, and brigades were not with their divisions. Communication and command broke down rapidly. The Yankees took advantage of the chaos to gradually sort through the mess, regroup and consolidate their units. Schofield then began a well organized fighting retreat and gradually disengaged his men from the fight.

As darkness fell, we found ourselves east of the Columbia Turnpike. The Yankees were on the west of the road and shifting to the north. What we didn't realize was that as the night wore on, Schofield shifted one regiment after another out of Columbia, past Spring Hill and up the road to Franklin. By daylight, even the last of the men at Spring Hill were gone. To our horror, the next morning the road revealed the passage of a large number of men. There were abandoned wagons, dead mules, and all types of debris in the road.

At one point, they had passed within one hundred yards of the closest Confederate skirmishers. They had heard troops passing on the road, but had thought they were Southern troops trying to relocate their units in the dark.

General Hood was furious that his plan had failed and Schofield had escaped the trap. He blamed everyone, including our own General Cleburne. Then to make matters worse, he accused General Granbury of cowardice. These hasty words, spoken in anger and later regretted, had a chilling effect on those of us who served under these two fine men. We knew they were some of the best leaders in Hood's Army of Tennessee. These men were heroes to us. For Hood to make such unjust accusations was beyond unfair. His claims of cowardice would have a profound effect. We had seen many terrible things in the war, but they would pale in comparison to what we were about to experience at Franklin, Tennessee.

17

November 24, 1864, Franklin, Tennessee

SCHOFIELD'S ARMY OF THE Cumberland had passed our very regiment in the night. We had thought it was Confederate General Brown's Division moving into position.

Ross's Cavalry Brigade had scouted ahead and returned a grim report. The small town of Franklin was positioned across the turnpike between Columbia and Nashville. It had been heavily fortified in 1863, and was situated in a curve of the Harpeth River. The Harpeth was too deep, wide and swift to be forded for miles in either direction. There was a railroad bridge behind Franklin, but it was passable by only a handful of men at a time who might cross on the rails. Schofield's men were already overlaying the tracks to make a plank road. The town was protected by two semi-circular earthworks extending from river bank to river bank. The outer work was thick, packed earth strengthened with logs. Field guns had been placed along the outer line. In front of the outer line was a deep wide ditch. Beyond the outer earthworks, two full brigades were deployed as skirmishers in a double line. The inner earthwork was similar to the outer, but a hundred yards back. It also bristled with field guns. To make matters even worse, across the river on a bluff overlooking Franklin, was Fort Granger. It mounted heavy artillery that controlled the approaches to Franklin and would be difficult, if not impossible, to silence without crossing the river.

––––––––

General Hood ordered an officers' call. All officers above the rank of captain were required to attend. He told them of his plan to sweep the Yankees into the Harpeth River with a massive frontal assault. An officers' call allows officers to speak freely in support or opposition to a commanding officer's plans, to point out strength and weaknesses of the plan, or make suggestions. Hood's plan was met with stark silence. Then, his corps commanders, one by one, expressed unanimous disapproval. They suggested finding a place downstream to cross, by-passing Franklin all together and making a run on the weakly defended ultimate goal of Nashville. Another suggested that a pontoon bridge could quickly be built, by-passing Franklin, or attacking it from its vulnerable back side. His divisional commanders expressed their concerns as well. No one spoke in support of the plan. He growled that Cleburne and Granbury had infected the others with their "shyness."

The officers returned to their units to explain the situation to their field officers. I was present when General Granbury explained things to the company commanders in the Texas Fifteenth Regiment, and to his friend, Captain Tyus, in particular.

"Ben, you know what this means. You're a fine soldier. Your men have given more than their share in this war. I will gladly assign your company or your whole regiment to be held in reserve. A lesser man than you would pack up and head for Texas. All I can ask is that you do your best."

"Sir, you and I have been friends for a long time. You know my Texas boys will do all that is asked of them, or die trying. As for the reserve unit duty, I thank you, but I'll decline. My men are frontline troops."

Word spread through camp like a horrible disease. We all knew that the next day would likely be the worst of the war that we had seen so far. Men wrote their names on pieces of paper and put them in their shoes, shirt and pants pockets. Noah, Pink and I did, too. Pink handed Noah a pocket watch that had been his father's along with fifteen silver dollars. "If anything happens to me tomorrow, please make sure your sister gets these."

"Shoot, Pink. You're about the most bullet proof soldier in the army. Ain't nothin' gonna happen to you, but I'll put it in with my stuff if you want me to."

That night, our platoon was bedded down much closer than usual. Everyone wanted to be near their family and friends. The Howards, Hunters, Rileys, Paytons, Andersons and Wades were in tight family clusters as were the three members of our family. Even Lieutenant Kinney and Trent rolled their beds out with our platoon. Justin Hunter played sad Irish tunes on his flute. We joined in singing softly when he played hymns. He played "A Mighty Fortress is our God" so sweetly there wasn't a dry eye around our fire.

Captain Tyus came by and talked to us. "I'm very proud to command you men. You have never let me down. Do your best tomorrow." He led us in a thoughtful prayer filled with emotion. It was the first time I ever remembered any of us praying together. I was scared, more scared than I had been at Fort Hindman; I was more scared than I had been at Pickett's Mill. As Captain Tyus prayed, great tears rolled down my cheeks as they did with many others. This time I knew what to expect and it was bad. I rolled out my bed between Pink and Noah. I needed to be close to them.

The morning of November 30 was clear and cold. Our breath

hung like steam in the still crisp air. General Hood got the Army of Tennessee into position the way he wanted and had us start advancing on Franklin. We stopped about a mile south of town. The Union skirmish lines were thick and easy to see. We were arranged in a long arc to match the earthworks. Hood assigned each division its place in the Confederate line. Stewart's Division formed the right flank. Brown's Division held the middle. Cleburne's Division formed the left flank. Granbury's Brigade anchored the left end of Cleburne's Division, with the Texas Fifteenth Regiment on the left end of Granbury's Brigade. That put Company F almost at the extreme left end of the entire line.

The guns of Fort Granger opened fire on us soon after we had formed our line. Their shots seemed to be falling long. I didn't know if it was out of fear of hitting their own skirmishers who were so near us, or if their guns would not depress any farther. Either way, I was glad. At three o'clock in the afternoon, Sul Ross's Seventh Texas Cavalry charged across the field and into the skirmishers. As the horsemen disrupted their line, the Yankees fell back and formed one heavy line. Once they did, the artillery from the fort found their range and began to do us some damage. Ross's Cavalry had to leave the field.

At half passed three in the afternoon, all of our regimental flags were unfurled. Ours, like several others, was still the Bonnie Blue Flag with its single star on a navy blue field. General Granbury and his staff dismounted and armed themselves with rifles, bayonets, and revolvers. He would personally lead his brigade. General Cleburne rode to each of his regimental commanders, then dismounted to fight near Granbury.

We advanced at the "double quick," raising the Rebel yell all along the front of the Army of Tennessee. Its familiar yelping steeled my heart for what was to come. My pulse quickened and my hands began to sweat in spite of the coolness of the day. Our battle cry was answered by the guns of Fort Granger. Bugles sounded and we charged. The two brigades of Yankee skirmishers fired their rifles, then ran for the safety of the earthworks. Many of them were too slow or stumbled. We cut them down with bayonets in their backs. While there were still Federal soldiers on the battlefield, the over-anxious gunners along the Union line opened fire with their cannon killing as many of their own men as they did ours. As we rushed the earthworks, cannon fired from only thirty yards away. The triple shotted load of canister struck like a giant sickle mowing down Clint, Joshua, Jonathan, Jordan, Justin and Jamison Hunter. I could see the flute in Justin's back pocket where he fell. Their voices were stilled that day, and the feet that had danced for joy so often would never move again.

Everything was a blur. I saw General Cleburne helping hoist men over the earthworks. Then he turned and grabbed his face. He had been shot through the head in the trench.

General Granbury was urging us on, firing his revolver at the enemy. A Yankee rifle shot him through the chest killing him instantly.

I don't remember how I got over the earthworks, but once inside, the Yankees were starting to fall back to their second line. I knelt and emptied my Spencer into their blue backs. The .56 caliber bullets claimed several Yankee lives. I reloaded and fired, reloaded and fired. Noah and Pink were near me doing the same thing. Once the retreating troops were out of the line of fire, the soldiers of the interior line opened on us with canister and rifle fire without ceasing. I saw brothers Will and Calvin Anderson go down together. They had fought bravely in every battle. Today, they had fought like wild bulls, slashing and tearing with their bayonets. They took a great many Yankees with them before they died.

Three regiments of Union troops came spilling out of the second line in a vigorous counterattack. We shot them down until they were right on top of us. I swung the butt of my empty Spencer into the throat of a charging Yankee. I hit him so hard, I broke his neck and the stock snapped off the barrel. The sheer weight of the counterattack pushed us back against the outer earthwork. Rifles fired and bayonets flashed all around me. I fired my LeMatt revolver until I had used all nine shots in the cylinder. I saw blood pouring from men I shot, but other soldiers immediately took their places. When I reached the outer earthwork, John Stone picked me up and hoisted me over the top, but a Yankee bayonet took his life. I stumbled in the ditch, trying to get on my feet. A Yankee appeared over the barricade with his rifle pointing at me. I fired the shotgun barrel of the LeMatt into his face from only feet away. Sergeant Harold Payton and his brother, Bradley, dragged me out of the ditch to safety.

Men in gray were standing in clusters, some bleeding, most looking for some kind of weapon. My Spencer rifle was broken and my LeMatt revolver was lost in the ditch. I found a Yankee Springfield rifle and a handful of cartridges under the body of a young dead Confederate soldier. As I searched his pockets for more cartridges or food, I realized it was my friend, Dane Carthel. The tall, skinny seventeen year old had died from a rifle ball to the head.

Sergeant Howard, Ham, Skeet and Ky were in the ditch. As Yankees reached over the earthwork to fire into it, Skeet and Ham would grab them by the wrists and pull them into the ditch as the others used their bayonets to kill them. Finally, so many rifles appeared at once, that the brave Sergeant and his three sons were all killed together. Corporal Riley sent his brother John to fetch more cartridges from the battlefield. He had not gone ten steps before he was shot dead through the back. Enraged, Corporal Riley struggled back over the barricade where he avenged his brother's life many times over, only to lose his own. I saw Lieutenant Kinney and Trent emerge from the ditch, covered with the blood of many man. They were shot down in the back as they tried to reach the small group of us assembling out of rifle range.

Night was falling and still we fought. I found Pink and Noah safe on the edge of the battlefield. Their faces were black with powder smoke and their coats were splattered with blood. We formed a little rifle company and moved in closer where we could shoot at Yankees on the earthworks. We used the bodies of the dead for protection. Pecos, Jake, and TJ Wade, Noah, Pink and I continued to fight under Sergeant Payton and his brother, Bradley. Recall sounded from the back of the battle field. We tried to work our way to the rear. A final volley from the Yankees cut down everyone but Pecos, Noah, Pink and me. When we got to the rear of the field we realized that the four of us were the only survivors from our whole platoon. We finally found Captain Tyus. Only nineteen men of the original one hundred and twenty men who had left Personville had survived.

During the night, Schofield's men began to leave Franklin for Nashville across the just completed road over the railroad bridge. No one tried to stop them. There were not enough of us left to do anything about it. Hood's Army of Tennessee had taken the field that morning with twenty-four thousand men. Only seven thousand men, including the walking wounded, were able to answer roll call that night. Seventeen thousand Confederate soldiers lost their lives at Franklin. That morning, Granbury's Brigade had taken the field with eleven hundred men. There were only three hundred and forty-four left alive. The Army of Tennessee was a shell of an army, a ghost of its former self.

Reality hit hard in the morning. We realized the Union troops had all escaped and were on their way to reinforce Nashville. And we realized that our army was gone. Six generals had died. Not a single general under General Hood remained; not a colonel, lieutenant colonel, or a major. The ranking officer left in Granbury's Brigade was Captain Tyus.

We dug trenches on either side of the road and laid the dead out two by two. There were so many dead men in the ditch in front of the earthwork that we collapsed the wall on top of them and buried them where they lay. Once more the road to glory had led to the gates of hell.

18

December 3, 1864, Nashville, Tennessee

WE HAD BURIED OUR DEAD at Franklin. We scavenged for weapons and cartridges from among their bodies and marched dejectedly on toward Nashville. The ghosts of Franklin haunted every step, as they would the rest of my life. I remembered when seventy thousand men in gray had proudly fought at Chickamauga. We had not been routed, for we had not fled the field. We had given all we had, but the Army of Tennessee had been dashed to pieces against the earthworks of Franklin defended by determined men.

When the tattered remnants of our forces reach Nashville, General Hood deployed an army that had already been beaten to death. He spread us out in a wide semi-circle. Schofield, and his now reinforced and well supplied army, waited for us in prepared defenses.

Our lines were stretched thin and our defenses were shallow trenches suitable only for firing while lying down. For shelter, we used fence rails to make a ridge pole and dried corn stalks as the walls and sides to at least slow the wind that howled from the north. We had very little food and scant ammunition.

The survivors of Granbury's Brigade and Cleburne's

Division were consolidated with other remnants into Cheatham's Division. Captain Tyus was now in command the three hundred men that remained of Granbury's Brigade. We found ourselves on the extreme right end of the Confederate line, up against the Murfreesboro Pike.

The weather was bitterly cold with freezing mist and sleet. On December 13, Captain Tyus received orders to construct a redoubt on the steep railroad cut where the Nashville and Chattanooga Railroad met the Murfreesboro Pike. The cut had been blasted out of solid rock, with sides that sloped down twenty feet, but made a natural defense on one side of the redoubt. The four sides were a palisade of stout logs with rifle ports. We cut logs and dugs holes, staggering through our work like dead men. We mounted four six pounder cannon through the walls and dug a deep trench in front of the three exposed sides. It gave us better protection from the weather than corn stalks and it was finished none too soon.

On the morning of December 15, Schofield ordered probing attacks against Hood's troops. Stedman's Federal Division attacked along the line of Cheatham's so called division. The Union troops included the United States Seventeenth Brigade, Colored Troops. We had never fought Negro troops before. Some of the men were very angry that these former slaves were taking up arms against us. At this point, I didn't see it made much difference and I just flat didn't care. Back home, some of the slaves over on the Brazos had been armed and fought in the militia along with the white men against the Indians and the Mexicans.

The fire from the redoubt and the thin line of Cheatham's men turned them back. The white troops of the Eighteenth Ohio Regiment tried their luck and died just as fast as the black men. The Second Battalion of the United States XIV Corps tried their luck and fled the field in disgrace. Our redoubt had held the Confederate right flank.

The Confederate left flank did not fare so well. The Union advance turned the flank and captured our small and only supply train. The Confederates were able to mount a fighting retreat. By dark, they had established themselves on Compton's Hill.

Hood pulled his army back almost three miles. The left wing was anchored on the slopes of Compton's Hill. The right end of the line rested on Overton Hill. We had to abandon our redoubt and move to support the Confederate left. We marched the length of the Confederate line in a freezing drizzle. Before we had even moved into line, we were ordered back to the right.

I was so cold and tired, I just tried to put one foot in front of the other. I stuck like a grass burr to Noah and Pink; after the nightmare at Franklin, I didn't want to be out of their sight. Once more, orders arrived that we were to return to support the Confederate center.

As the weak rays of morning tried to penetrate the damp gray skies, we found ourselves just marching up to the center. The Union troops renewed their assault against Overton Hill on our right. Believing this was the main attack, Hood pulled us out of line and sent at the double to support Lowery's Alabama Brigade. We found ourselves facing the Negro troops of Steedman's Division. They attacked us like men, and fought as well as any soldiers we had faced. But they died just as well, too. We repelled their attack before they ever reached our lines.

I was so exhausted that it was difficult to hold my rifle steady. My breathing came in deep gasps. I would not have been able survive close combat. I was simply too tired. If it came to that, they could just kill me. I was too tired to run. We got a reprieve as the attack against the right flank sputtered to a stop.

The fighting was far from over. Schofield had intended the attack against the right to draw men away from his main attack on the Confederate left flank on Compton's Hill. General Thomas, the "Rock of Chickamauga", directed a ringing hammer blow against the gentle slope. The tattered, shivering men from Tennessee were overwhelmed by sheer numbers of Union troops. They collapsed back against Ector's Texas Brigade. The Texans held the line as it curved back under the weight of the attack.

Union cavalry managed to get behind the Texans and attacked them from the rear. The line broke and the gray-clad men ran for their lives. As the left collapsed, the center gave way to a Federal frontal attack. The weary Confederate soldiers found the strength to run from the crashing blue wave.

The remnants of the right flank tried to mount a fighting retreat. But a Union battery of horse artillery wheeled into view and began pouring a hot fire into the rear guard. All was lost. We were routed and ran from the Yankee cannon.

Ector's Brigade was able to organize enough of a defense to allow the rest of us to escape. Their bravery cost them dearly. Of the five hundred and sixty-nine men in Ector's Brigade who marched into Nashville, only one hundred and eighty-four would ever leave.

I stumbled down the cold muddy road. My only thought was escaping the pursuing Yankee cavalry. General Forrest's weary Confederate cavalry stung the Yankees hard enough that they temporarily ended their deadly assault. The skies opened with steady freezing rain, soaking us to the bone. We gradually slowed to a walk as the mud pulled at our freezing feet. I hoped that the rain at least hid my tears.

19

December 17, 1864, Franklin, Tennessee

ON DECEMBER 17, WE HAD retreated as far as Franklin, Tennessee, a place I had hoped never to see again. We shared whatever hard tack and jerky we had, but it wasn't much. Our officers got us sorted out in some semblance of order by mid-morning.

We attacked the small garrison force at Fort Granger. Their guns were sighted toward the river and town below. It was a simple thing to overwhelm the men there. We disarmed them and set them on the road to meet General Schofield, who we knew was not too far behind. We spiked the guns where they could not easily be used against us again.

We crossed the plank bridge into Franklin and burned it behind us. We camped that night between the inner and outer earthworks. We built fires with boards pulled off of houses and wooden fence rails. We scoured the devastated town for anything to eat without much luck. The local citizens had still not returned from the earlier battle. The stench of the recently buried soldiers hung over the place. Only when the wind shifted directions did we get relief from the horrible smell. There was nothing left to scavenge here, just broken weapons and ruined clothes. The ghosts of the battlefield walked at night, disturbing my sleep. I lay awake remembering that horrible day when so many of my friends had died until exhaustion finally gave way to dream tormented sleep.

We headed on south as fast as our weary underfed cold bodies would take us. I walked between Pink and Noah. The Confederate cavalry kept a screen between us and the pursuing Union troops. At a place called Sugar Creek, near the Tennessee River, we assumed a defensive position along a ridge and showed the Yankee vanguard that, although this dog was whipped, it still had teeth. They pulled back in their pursuit and allowed us to cross the Tennessee River on December 26, 1864, into the relative safety of northern Alabama on the same pontoon bridge we had crossed months before.

The cavalry left us there. They had orders for raids into parts of Alabama and Mississippi. News caught up with us. Abraham Lincoln had been re-elected President of the United States. There was now no hope for a new President from the Peace Party to end the war. It would be a fight to the death. Savannah had fallen. Sherman was preparing to work his way north through the Carolinas and join forces with Grant in Virginia. We continued to work our way deeper to the south and west. On New Year's Eve, we found ourselves in Iuka, Mississippi.

"Pink. Noah. This is the closest we been to Texas in almost three years. The Army of Tennessee is out of the war. What do you think about us headin' home?"

"We sure done our duty, and then some, to the South. Maybe Aaron's right. What do you think about it, Pink?"

"You boys go on home if you want to; I sure don't see anything wrong with it. I'm waitin' to see what Captain Tyus does. If he goes home, by gum, I'm goin', too. But if he stays, I'm stayin'."

Pecos had been listening to our conversation. "All the family I got is dead now, layin' up there at Franklin. I haven't got anywhere to go, so if y'all don't care, I reckon I'll just stick with you." We decided maybe Pink was right. At least we had cornmeal and bacon again.

On January 17, 1865, General P.G.T. Beauregard of Louisiana

arrived to relieve General Hood. He had never been the same since the slaughter at Franklin. General Beauregard said they were gathering up all the stray units like ours to put together into a new army under the command of none other than General Joseph Johnston himself. The army would try to work its way to Virginia and join up as reinforcements for General Lee. Captain Tyus joined up. With the Captain going, and Johnston as our commander, it was not hard to join with them.

We marched back across Alabama and cut the corner up into South Carolina. Noah reminded me that our father was born in Marlboro County over in northeast South Carolina. We both wondered if we still had family there. We were placed into a mixed bunch of odds and ends called the First Texas Infantry. As usual, we were short on food, clothes and shelter, but dangerously short on ammunition. But truth be told, we were pretty short on fight, too.

At Bentonsville, North Carolina, we turned to fight a detached part of Sherman's army. We repelled the first attack. The Yankees regrouped and prepared to attack again. But our ammunition had been expended in the first assault. As the Yankees got close enough we began to throw rocks at them. The Federals were so shocked that they stopped and began to laugh. We broke and ran away like rabbits from a pack of hounds.

On April 2, 1865, the Confederate defenses at Petersburg, Virginia fell. General Robert E. Lee, commander of the Army of Northern Virginia, evacuated Richmond. The Confederate government fled in panic. On April 9, General Lee, the most revered Confederate leader, surrendered his army to General Ulysses S. Grant at Appomattox Courthouse. Grant was generous in victory. He allowed the officers to keep their side arms, and the men were allowed to take a horse or mule so they could try to put in a crop when they got home. When the news reached us, we knew the war was over.

A madman, angry at the defeat of the South, and fervent hater of President Lincoln, shot him in the head at Ford's Theater in Washington. He died the morning of April 15. Andrew Johnson was sworn in as President that same day. Sentiment for a peaceful reconciliation died with the President. The people of the North were furious. The Union soldiers were demanding vengeance. We knew we couldn't withstand another attack. But, we were afraid if we surrendered we might be killed.

General Johnston had already begun surrender talks with General Sherman. Both realized that this turn of events had changed things. Sherman offered the same terms Grant had given to Lee. Johnston surrendered April 26, 1865. Our days of serving under "Uncle Joe" had ended. The war was over for us.

_____

I didn't feel especially sad. I guess I was more relieved. I couldn't find enough emotion to either laugh or cry. I just felt numb except for one painful emotion. I wanted to go home.

A list of our names was made out in duplicate, indicating we had surrendered. We were each issued a warrant of parole in which we agreed not to take up arms against the United States. It would serve as our passport home. Grant and Sherman remained conciliatory toward the surrendered soldiers of the former Confederacy. They counseled their extremely loyal troops that these men were to be treated with respect and generosity. Their anger over Lincoln's death did not spill over on us.

_____

The Yankees opened up their commissaries and fed and clothed us well. I didn't care that the pants and coat were blue. They gave us new wool blankets and factory made brogans. We had all the beans, pork and cornbread we could eat. Everybody was allowed a cup of coffee in the morning. I needed all these things and appreciated them. But I wanted to go home.

We were divided into groups depending on our destinations as we waited for transportation home. We stayed in new canvas tents and slept on cots. The guards treated us more like old friends than enemies. They made sure we had everything we needed. They told us their names and where they were from. We swapped stories with them and other Confederate veterans as we waited impatiently to go home.

Word came that we were to leave soon. The night before we were to leave, Captain Tyus found us. He would be going home to Texas, too. His home was near Waco, and he hoped we would find the time to see him. He told us what good soldiers we had been and how proud he was of us. His eyes glazed over with tears as he shook hands with each of us. When he got to me, I hugged his neck and we both started crying.

"Captain Tyus, my daddy died when I was a baby, so I never knew him. I reckon you've been as good to me as any daddy. I won't ever forget you."

"I won't ever forget you, Aaron, or you, Pecos, Noah, or Pink. Some of you came to me as boys and are going home as men. I lost my own son in this war. You boys are the only sons I have left. I really do hope you'll come see me and my wife. My home is open to you any time."

He turned to leave, but Pecos called out for him to wait. "Platoon, attention! Salute!" We drew ourselves to rigid attention and snapped sharp salutes. Captain Tyus smiled, then looked serious as he returned our salute.

———————

A train took us in clean boxcars to Wheeling, West Virginia. Here they checked our papers and put us on steam transports. We steamed down the Ohio for days, taking in the sights through eyes that would never see the world the same way again.

At Cairo, Illinois, there was some sorting out to do, but after one night on shore we were headed down the Mississippi to Port Hudson, Louisiana. They sorted us again and by the next day we were steaming up the Red River to Natchitoches. Here they allowed us to draw for a horse or mule to take us home. As we didn't know what waited for us at home, all of us drew mules except Pecos. He said he'd rather walk than ride a mule.

"Where you gonna go, Pecos? Me and Noah would sure like to have you stay a while with us at Navasota Crossing. We got a big house, lots of farm land, and plenty of livestock."

"Well, I'll try it and if the company and grub ain't too bad I might stick around."

The three mules and one horse weren't much to brag about. They had been used hard and were thin. But a little rest, some good care and feed and they would serve our purposes. I spent a little of my money to buy us a skillet, some bacon and cornmeal for the trip, and a bag of oats for the animals. We left at daylight heading west on the old Camino Real, the same road my father had taken the first time he came to Texas. Although we had to ride bareback, we got to the Sabine River just at sunset. Pink, yellow and gold shone through the cottonwood trees and reflected off the stained water. As I splashed my mule across the waters of the Sabine I felt a chill up and down my spine. This was Texas! I was home!

This was the very crossing where my father had first entered Texas and fallen under her spell. Now I was making that same journey, returning to my native state. I had sought the road to glory and found that nothing could be more glorious than the road to home.

20

May 28, 1865, Navasota Crossing, Texas

WE PUSHED ON DOWN THE Camino Real as fast as our tired animals and our sore rear ends would allow. We rode into Navasota Crossing at just full dark. We could see light in the kitchen of our house. We dismounted and headed for the back porch, except for Pecos, who tended the livestock.

We climbed onto the porch and knocked on the back door. Mary Ann opened the door cautiously with the barrel of a shotgun pointing at our bellies. "Who are you and what do you want?"

"Mary Ann?"

"Pinckney!"

He grabbed her up and whirled her around in his arms on the porch. Momma stepped out on the porch to see what all the fuss was about.

"Momma, Pinckney is home with some friends."

Our hair was long and shaggy, but still red. Noah had a short red untrimmed beard, but I didn't have a whisker. I had been twelve when we left and Noah had been fourteen. Now we were fifteen and seventeen. I was six foot four inches, an inch taller than Noah. We just looked at Momma and smiled.

"How can I help you boys?"

"Don't you know your own sons, Momma?"

"Thank the Lord, it's Aaron and Noah. You've got to be Noah with the whiskers!" She burst into tears. We both hugged her at the same time, crying right along with her. I've been praying for you boys to come home safe since Sixty-two. Thank God you're home! Is that David out there at the stables? David, come up here."

"Momma, that's not David. That's our friend, Pecos Wade. David died of pneumonia while we were in that prison camp in Chicago. We sent a letter. I guess you didn't get it."

She turned to cry into her apron. "Did you get my letter about Alma? She died after having Alice. This little girl is her."

A sandy haired little toddler peeked around Momma's skirts. "Hello, Alice. I'm Uncle Aaron. This is Uncle Noah." She just hid farther into her skirts. "Something sure smells good in the kitchen!"

"All I got is some kinda tough beef steaks to fry, cornbread and a big pot of mustard greens."

Beef and something green to eat, fresh butter for the cornbread and all the buttermilk I could drink. I thought I was going to eat until I popped. Pink would hardly turn loose of Mary Ann long enough to eat. Everybody made Pecos feel welcome.

There was so much I wanted to tell Mother, and much to hide from her. I found myself thinking things through before I told them, skipping some details and cleaning up the stories to make them less objectionable. I hadn't done anything for which I was ashamed, and had done some things for which I was proud. But for most of them, Mother didn't need to know all the details. Some I just wanted to forget, and some I never would. I told her in a general way about the battles we had won and lost, the prison camp, and David's death there. I told her about the places I had been and the interesting things I had seen.

There were plenty of things I had seen I would never tell to anyone except Noah, Pink and Pecos. I told her about the food we ate, including horse and mule. She laughed and said she had eaten both lots of times when she and my father had first come to Texas.

She told us about the crops, livestock and local news. Mary Ann and Pink slipped off upstairs earlier than the rest of us. They would move back to their own cabin soon, but tonight they were here together. Noah and I just grinned at each other, and Pecos pretended not to notice. We finally went to bed; Momma put Noah and me back in our old room. It had two beds now instead of one. It was a good thing since we had both grown quite a bit since we left. I couldn't image not sharing a room with Noah. We were even closer than when we left in '62. He would be the best friend I ever had. Mother offered Pecos the other room with a bed to himself. He was glad to accept. I lay awake in bed a long time, listening to Noah snoring a little in the other bed. The sounds and smells of the house reassured me I was home at last.

———

I hadn't really understood why there was a war when I left home in 1862 at age twelve. Now, three long, bloody years later, I still did not understand why we had fought. I knew the reasons I had heard and been told a thousand times, but I still was not convinced that any of the reasons justified what had happened, all the men and boys who had died, or come home missing arms or legs. I learned soon enough that Yankees were folks just like us. I had killed when I had to, and there had been plenty of folks trying to kill me. I had lost a big brother who had been like a father to me, and lost more friends than I could count. I had become even closer to Noah, and had come to consider Pink just like a brother. I had met men that I looked up to and would never forget the influence they had on me. Captain Tyus had become a father figure to me in many ways. I had spent time in a prison camp. I had been in small skirmishes and huge battles. I had known the taste of both victory and defeat. There were horrible images that were forever seared in my memory.

I had been enticed by the bright flags, patriotic speeches, military music and uniforms to strike out with my brothers on the greatest adventure of our lives. We left Texas together on the road to glory. But I had found hell on earth. I had learned not to be afraid.

I understood the value of friends who would die for one another without a thought. Great pleasure could be had in simple things like a shared joke or a cup of hot coffee. Through the talents of the Hunter family, I had found how music could move me to joy or tears. I had learned to depend on my own abilities, and how to handle myself in the world of men and the hell of war.

I had left Navasota Landing as a boy and returned as a man. But the things that I had seen and heard and done had changed me in a way that only someone who had experienced the same things could understand, and I was not sure that I would ever understand them myself. I had set my feet on the road to glory and found that it led to death, destruction and the gaping open gates of hell.

Epilogue

AARON, NOAH, AND PINCKNEY did return in 1865 as changed men. Aaron would be known his whole life as a man who could take whatever the world could throw at him with honesty, self-reliance and courage. He would know a widely varied life as cowboy, farmer, merchant, postmaster, freighter, and livery owner. He would survive the very difficult years of Reconstruction in Texas, the era of the great cattle drives and the arrival of the Dust Bowl and Great Depression.

In 1938, at age eighty-eight, he was invited to the Seventy-fifth Reunion of Civil War Veterans held at Gettysburg, Pennsylvania. All veterans, both Union and Confederate, from all theaters of the war, were invited to attend. Aaron was provided round trip train tickets from Brownfield, Texas, to Gettysburg. He stayed the full eight days of the reunion. When he returned, something within him had changed. He was finally able to talk about his war experiences with his family. The trip seemed to provide him a healing relief of the burdens that he had carried for seventy-five years. He died six months later at peace with God and himself.

Aaron's mother, Nancy, was a remarkable woman. She outlived three husbands. She gave birth to a dozen children, only to see many of them buried. She was still alive and living with her son, Marcus King, in the 1880 census. She kept her promise and raised her granddaughter, Alice.

Mary Ann and Pinckney Hawkins lived long and successful lives in Limestone County where their descendants still live.

Noah was alive to sign the deed with Aaron and his mother when they sold their land in Leon County in 1870. He married in 1872 in Freestone County. What became of him remains a mystery. David Turner is buried in a mass grave on Confederate Mound, Oak Lawn Cemetery, in Chicago, where he was buried in 1863.

Many of the historical characters in this work of historical fiction were true Texas heroes. Granbury and Cleburne both have towns named in their honor. Sul Ross returned to Texas where he served as Governor and as President of Texas A&M University. While his battle tactics are controversial to some, no one can deny the courage and tenacity of John Bell Hood, who remains a venerated Texas hero.

The story of Aaron Lloyd Turner's long and adventurous life in Texas will be chronicled in three future volumes. *Up from the Ashes* follows Aaron's struggles to deal with the injustice of Reconstruction and his experiences on the Shawnee and Chisholm Trails. *On the Western Trail* tells the story of Aaron's adventures along the Great Western Trail, the coming of the railroad and the establishment of his family ranching and freighting enterprises at the western edge of civilization in Texas. *The Last Trail West* tells of Aaron's last move west, up onto the arid south plains of Texas. He and his family will confront Spanish influenza, drought, the Great Depression and the Dust Bowl. Aaron will finally make peace with his memories from the Civil War.

Glossary

Back strap: the choicest cuts of meat from along the backbone.

Black gumbo: a type of notoriously heavy black clay soil.

Brogans: heavy leather plain work shoes.

Canister: a type of artillery shell that contains large numbers of iron musket balls.

Constitutional Union Party: a short-lived political party from about 1856-60; party was pro-slavery; pro-states' rights, and strongly supported preserving the Union; Sam Houston was a prominent leader.

Contraband: a prohibited product; the spoils of war which the victor may claim; a term for freed slaves who followed Union troops.

Corps: a subunit of a larger army containing three or more divisions; at full strength, a corps represented 30,000 or more men; they rarely fought at full strength and were often far smaller.

Cracker: slang term for poor white rural Southerner.

Dysentery: severe infectious diarrhea.

Gangrene: a serious wound infection that requires amputation of the affected limb to save the patient.

Grape shot: an artillery round continuing many one pound iron shot.

Grippe: an obsolete term for a variety of respiratory infections with fever, especially the flu.

Haunch: the hindquarters of a butchered animal.

Irish flute: a wooden or metal flute played straight out or down from the mouth similar to a recorder.

Latrine: outdoor toilets.

Legion: a type of military unit that was already becoming obsolete by the time of the Civil War containing infantry, cavalry and artillery.

Lye soap: soap made with rendered animal fat, usually hog lard and lye; lye is strongly alkaline and could be made by soaking wood ashes in water.

Picket: a rope to which horses are tied when not in use to keep them from straying; also, a term for a soldier on guard duty.

Platoon: a military unit of roughly twenty enlisted men under the supervision of a lieutenant, two sergeants and four corporals; usually divided into two squads under each of the sergeants.

Pontoon bridge: a bridge built across floating structures, often especially designed boats.

Quartermaster: an officer in charge of food and military supplies.

Redoubt: a fortified military position.

Rim fire: a type of self-contained cartridge that contains the explosive charge around the rim of the cartridge case.

Salvo: a simultaneous discharge of an artillery battery.

Skedaddle: a slang term for running away.

Skirmish: a minor military conflict.

Skirmishers: soldiers placed in advance of the main line; their function was to alert the main body of an approaching enemy, and to slow and disorganize their approach.

Slop bucket, slop jar: a container for human waste.

Squad: a subdivision of a platoon under the control of a sergeant and two corporals, usually consisting of ten men.

Vanguard: the leading unit of an advancing body of troops.

War bag: a heavy waterproofed canvas or leather bag for carrying essential items such as food and ammunition and extra clothes.

Military Organization at the Time of the American Civil War

Military Units in Descending Organizational Strength:

Army: Usually under the Command of a General or Lieutenant General; usually contained three of or more corps; ideally an army would contain 90,000 men or many more at full strength, although they rarely fought at full strength.

Corps: Usually under command of a Lieutenant General or Major General; usually contained three or more divisions with a total of 30,000 or more men at full strength.

Division: Usually under the command of a Major General or Brigadier General; usually contained three or more brigades; theoretically contained 10,000 men.

Brigade: Usually under the command of a Brigadier General or a Colonel; contained three or more regiments; at full strength a unit of 3,000 men.

Regiment: Usually under the command of a Colonel, Lieutenant Colonel or Major; a regiment was the basic unit of the whole army; they were often recruited from the same area and were often related; a regiment might contain ten or more companies; they usually contained 1,000 or more men when at full strength, which rarely occurred; regiments were usually fiercely loyal to their commanding officer, and very much tied to their home state; they frequently were named for their commanding officer and home state.

Company: Usually recruited from the same town or county; the men often knew each other and were often related; they often elected their captains, and other officers; theoretically contained 100 men plus officers; by the end of the war, they may have been reduced to a handful of men.

Platoon: Unit under the command of a Lieutenant or First Lieutenant consisting of twenty enlisted men, two sergeants, and four corporals.

Squad: Basic unit under one sergeant and two corporals; roughly ten men.

Ranks of Military Personnel in Descending Order:

General, Lieutenant General, Major General,
Brigadier General, Colonel, Lieutenant Colonel, Major,
Captain, First Lieutenant, Second Lieutenant,
Sergeant (various types and ranks),
Corporal, Private.

Weapons:

The basic Union weapon was the Springfield muzzle loading rifle. It was approximately 47" long and most commonly fired a .58 caliber bullet, although in the field it was often referred to as a .50 caliber. Paper cartridges for it were interchangeable with the very similar Confederate Enfield rifle, imported from England. Both we fitted with a bayonet.

A number of lever action rifles were used by the Union, especially the Spencer and the Henry. They used rim fire breech loading metal cartridges. The South had no means to manufacture ammunition for these guns, so scavenging became very important. They appeared more commonly in the western armies.

The basic revolvers were six-shot Colt Navy and Army revolvers in .36 and .44 caliber, with the .44 being much more common. An unusual weapon was manufactured in New Orleans, the LeMatt nine shot revolver. It fired a .44 cartridge, but the center pin of the revolver was a 20 gauge shotgun barrel. These guns were expensive officers' weapons of fierce fire power which sometimes found their way into the hands of lucky enlisted men.

Artillery consisted of field artillery and heavy artillery. Field artillery could be moved into position by horses and generally ranged from the common twelve pounders to nine, six and four pounders. The four and six pounders were often referred to as light artillery or horse artillery. Heavy artillery referred to guns larger than twelve pounders, ranging up to one hundred pound shells. Artillery shells were anti-personnel such as canister and grape shot, or common solid shot. Exploding shells were often used in heavy guns. Mortars were seen at sieges. They could throw enormous shells at high trajectories over defenses and explode over the heads of troops to devastating effects.

Camp Stephen Douglas, Chicago Illinois:

An eighty acre prisoner of war camp set in swampy land near Chicago. Early in the war, prisoners seemed to receive relatively humane care. As the war progressed, it became notorious for its horrible conditions. It was sometimes referred to as "The Andersonville of the North." Many prisoners died of disease, starvation, and exposure to the elements.

Suggested Reading

Campbell, Randolph B. *Gone to Texas: a history of the Lone Star State*. New York: Oxford University Press, 2003.

Catton, Bruce. *This Hallowed Ground*. New York: Doubleday and Company, 1956.

Coggins, Jack. *Arms and Equipment of the Civil War*. New York: Doubleday and Company, 1962.

Fehrenbach, T. R. *Lone Star: A History of Texas and Texans*. New York: Collier Books, 1968

Lundberg, John R. *The Finishing Stroke: Texans in the 1864 Tennessee Campaign*. Abilene, Texas: McWhiney Foundation Press, 2002

Genealogy

Thomas Turner, Ireland, circa 1732; died SC, 1796; = Priscella Alexander, Ireland

Thomas Turner, Jr., Marlboro Co., SC, 1751; died Marlboro Co., SC, 1822 = Rebekah (last name not recorded)

Aaron Turner, Marlboro Co., SC, 1783; died Leon Co., TX December 18, 1851 = Nancy King, GA

Aaron Lloyd Turner, Leon Co., TX, December 17, 1850; died Brownfield, Terry Co., TX, February 22, 1939 = Ella Fisher, TX

John Karr Turner, Moro, Taylor Co., TX, December 12, 1890; died Seagraves, Gaines Co., TX, June 1, 1964 = Effie Beatrice Smith, MO

Aaron Lynn Turner, Seagraves, Gaines Co., TX, May 2, 1931 = Doris Alene Combs, Madison Co., AR

Stephen Lynn Turner, Fayetteville, Washington Co., AR, January 10, 1957; = Roberta Ann Lyles, Baton Rouge, East Baton Rouge Parrish, LA

Melissa Ruth Turner, Lubbock, Lubbock Co., TX, September 12, 1984 = Dustin Alan DeBusk, TX
Aaron Lyles Turner, Plainview, Hale Co., TX, January 19, 1988 = Sarah M. Robinson, TX